Having written over eighty-five novels, **Tara Taylor Quinn** is a *USA TODAY* bestselling author with more than seven million copies sold. She is known for delivering intense, emotional fiction. Tara is a past president of Romance Writers of America. She has won a Readers' Choice Award and is a seven-time finalist for an RWA RITA® Award. She has also appeared on TV across the country, including CBS Sunday Morning. She supports the National Domestic Violence Hotline. If you or someone you know might be a victim of domestic violence in the United States, please contact 1-800-799-7233.

Also by Tara Taylor Quinn

Wife by Design
Once a Family
Husband by Choice
Child by Chance
Mother by Fate
The Good Father
Love by Association

Discover more at millsandboon.co.uk

HER LOST
AND FOUND
BABY

TARA TAYLOR QUINN

MILLS & BOON

First Published in Great Britain 2018
by Mills & Boon, an imprint of HarperCollins*Publishers*
1 London Bridge Street, London, SE1 9GF

Her Lost and Found Baby © 2018 TTQ Books, LLC

ISBN: 978-0-263-26520-0

0818

MIX
Paper from
responsible sources
FSC® C007454

This book is produced from independently certified FSC™
paper to ensure responsible forest management.

For more information visit: www.harpercollins.co.uk/green

Printed and bound in Spain
by CPI, Barcelona

To My Harlequin Family, Thank You.

Chapter One

Hot stuff.

Johnny Brubaker squeezed his eyes shut and didn't open them again until he knew all he'd see were the cardboard bowls side-by-side on the food truck's long prep area in front of him.

He looked at the tickets hanging from the thin rack mounted above the board. He scooped rice, black beans and green beans, then added onion, lettuce and a healthy squirt of his signature barbecue-ranch dressing. He capped the first bowl, put the ticket on top of it and moved to the second. This one needed steak. The next was pork. He finished with all three in under a minute, keeping his line of vision completely under control.

Until a customer at the window of his food truck, Angel's Food Bowls, asked a question of the woman taking orders.

"Johnny?" Tabitha Jones, the pediatric nurse who helped him on her days off, called out, naturally drawing his gaze.

And there was that sweet butt again. How had it gotten so cute overnight? Six months they'd been doing this, on and off, almost nine months of being neighbors and becoming friends, and *now* he was noticing her in that way?

"Yeah?" He turned back to his bowls, aware of the male face peering at him through the window but not caring all that much. They'd been parked on a public thoroughfare by San Diego's Mission Beach for more than three hours, and he'd had people peering at him through that window ever since.

"The health inspector would like to know if he can board the truck." Tabitha's voice held a hint of...a less than upbeat tone.

Damn. "Of course he can board," Johnny said, glancing at the truck's order window with a mostly sincere smile on his face. He wanted a surprise inspection about as much as the next guy—never—but as an attorney, he knew that the more proven compliance records he amassed, the less vulnerable he'd be to a lawsuit.

The world was full of crazies and he'd discovered that jealousy ran rampant in the food-truck business.

Besides, they had a long line, and a more than thirty-second wait per customer could cause folks to wander away. He'd rather have the inspector in the truck if it meant he could possibly keep business going.

Taking a second to reach into the bin above the driver's-side visor, he pulled out the portfolio of plastic page protectors, all filled with the various permits and licenses he'd had to acquire, and set it on the driver's seat of the truck. Then, stopping at the small sink designated only for handwashing, he squirted liquid soap on both hands. He lathered up to his elbows, in between his fingers and on the top of his hands, rinsed, dried himself on a disposable towel and, donning a new pair of plastic gloves, returned to work.

Pretending he hadn't passed by Tabitha's backside twice in the process.

What was with him?

Having his mind wander while engaged in a successful project—that he understood. Seemed to be his life story. But to look at Tabitha and see… To look at her that way, it just wasn't right.

And it wasn't like him, either.

They were partners in grief. Helping each other out with "life quest" projects, as she called them. Things they had to do so they could get on with the rest of their lives.

They were each other's shoulder to cry on, propping each other up when necessary.

But they were not sexual beings. They'd both sworn off it until their quests were done. Their friendship was a safe zone. Tabitha's drive to find her missing two-year-old son took up whatever emotional and physical energy she had left after the duties of her days. And Johnny…he was honoring his dead wife. You didn't do that by sleeping with another woman.

He didn't kid himself into thinking he'd never be open to a relationship again. He was only thirty—and alive. Alex Brubaker, Johnny's father, expected a grand-heir to the family dynasty; Johnny wanted to raise one. But the food truck had been Angel's passion.

It was his way of making sense of the fact that she'd died so young—senselessly murdered in a robbery over a year ago. If the guy, who'd taken a plea deal to avoid life without parole, had just asked for her purse, for her ATM card, she'd have handed them over. Money hadn't been that important to her.

Angel hadn't wanted the food truck as a means of earning cash for herself. She'd planned to donate all the proceeds to charity. Just as Johnny was doing. She'd loved to cook for people. Had loved the idea of traveling around from place to place and being just another person on the beach, working hard like everyone else.

As the daughter of a wealthy oilman and a graduate of one of the country's most elite culinary institutes, she'd been able to open her own five-star restaurant where she cooked elegant dinners for some of the country's most powerful people. And she'd been in the limelight, on the food channels, being written up in gourmet magazines.

But her real dream had been the food truck. She'd died before it could happen. So, to honor Angel, Johnny was taking a year out of his life to do it for her.

Getting involved with another woman didn't belong anywhere in that plan.

"Everything looks good."

Johnny nodded, barely glancing up from his bowls as the skinny fortysomething inspector spoke from the back of the truck. He was pleased to have the inspector leave positive paperwork for the portfolio. And to see the line still snaking out from the truck. This was the first of four days he and Tabitha would spend here, an hour and a half south of their Mission Viejo homes, and they'd have to make enough this first day—Sunday—to compensate for the smaller crowds and shorter hours on the weekdays.

The truck, his mission, was important, but they'd parked it in San Diego specifically so Tabitha could check out yet another daycare. She was certain this time.

He was, too. Certain that she was setting herself up for one more disappointment. Her goal—finding her son—mattered more than any food truck. He wanted it for her way more than he wanted his own success. He was just finding it harder, after months on the road with her, to keep his hope up on her behalf. But he'd do his part. Help her by playing the "dad" in a couple checking out daycares for their daughter. Just as Tabitha was helping him with the truck. It was the deal they'd made.

That thought came with an involuntary glance in her

direction. She was leaning over the counter to hand his most recent creation—a bowl with only rice, onions, meat and dressing—out the window, putting her butt right before his eyes…again. Her jeans had jewels on the pockets. He'd never noticed jewels on her pockets before. Must be new. And that had to be the reason he was suddenly liking a part of Tabitha he had no business noticing.

Yep, had to be the jewels.

Weak, at best, but the explanation was all he had, so he was going with it.

The Bouncing Ball Daycare was located on the ground floor of one of San Diego's nicer professional buildings. There was nothing opulent or ostentatious about the place, but judging by the placards on the walls and the cars in the lot on a Monday morning, the various small businesses and law firms that occupied the space were successful. One company, Braden Property Management, took up the entire top floor, according to a sign out front.

Tabitha homed in on the immaculate green grass and colorful flower beds that greeted them as they approached. Went inside.

"Didn't you say the daycare owner's name is Mallory Harris?" Johnny asked.

Fighting the tremors that assailed her any time she thought she might be close to Jackson, Tabitha stood in front of the directory in the building's lobby and tried to focus on Johnny's words.

Something about the daycare owner. Her name. Mallory Harris.

"Yes," she said, equally grateful for and bothered by his innocuous interruption. Suspecting he'd done it on purpose, to distract her from the emotions assailing her, she was mostly grateful.

That day almost nine months before, when Johnny Brubaker had moved into the tiny house next to hers a mile from the beach in Mission Viejo, had been the second-best day of her life. Following Jackson's birth, which had been the best.

The absolute worst had been the day Jackson's biological father had failed to return him to her...

Johnny had purchased the little house as step one in his attempt to bring his murdered wife's dream to life. Angel had wanted to leave their elite, moneyed, always-in-the-spotlight life behind and live like a "normal" person.

Looking up into Johnny's clear blue eyes calmed Tabitha unlike anything else. His easy acceptance of... everything somehow made life seem more manageable. "You ready?" she asked.

"Whenever you are." His voice held the usual note of confidence, leaving her with the feeling that he'd stand there in front of the directory all day if she needed him to, no questions asked.

But she knew he'd need a break. Johnny wasn't good about missing his meals—not that you'd ever be able to tell he had a voracious appetite by looking at him. All six feet of the man were rock solid.

He waited for her to lead the way. She'd chosen her outfit carefully—a flowing summer skirt, brightly colored with small flowers, a ribbed T-shirt to match and sandals. She'd chosen his, too, because he'd asked—casual dark shorts and a light green button-up shirt—also with sandals. Johnny's real life, the one he'd be going back to when his sabbatical was over, required suits and ties.

But for running a food truck...not such a good idea.

Early on in their friendship, he'd asked her to go with him to buy a more casual wardrobe.

She'd laughed out loud that day for the first time since Jackson had been stolen away from her.

"I think this is it." Johnny spoke just behind her.

While the daycare took up a lot of the first floor, the door leading into it was one panel with a small window at the top. Nothing there to invite strangers into the midst of the children. And no windows through which she could look from the outside. She knew the place had windows, plenty of them. She'd pored over the establishment's website. First, so she'd seem like a parent who really was interested in a place for her child. And second, so she'd be fully prepared for whatever she'd have to come up with to gain access to one particular child. Hers.

Legal access, of course. The police would help when she had something valid to bring them. Detective Bentley, her contact back home in Mission Viejo, had assured her that no matter how much time passed, he'd keep looking. He just needed something to go on.

"You have to turn that knob there for the door to open." Johnny's droll tone was completely lacking in the sarcasm his comment might have suggested. The steady kindness she'd come to associate with him was out in full force.

"I know," she told him, afraid to turn around, afraid she'd be tempted to hide in the warmth of his gaze, put her head on his shoulder and cry. Because she was afraid that when she opened the door, the hope that had been keeping her going all week would be dashed.

And because... What if Jackson *was* behind that door and she'd finally, after over a year, hold her baby in her arms again?

It wouldn't happen immediately. There'd be red tape.

Still…her heart felt as though it might burst at the thought of seeing him and she consciously moved on, thinking of the nursery she'd changed into a bedroom for a toddler over the past year.

She'd done it with Johnny's help, when he had the time and was alone in the evenings, too. She'd made wall hangings, a comforter and furry stuffed pillows in the shapes of animals.

She finally turned the knob, recalling the photo she'd found on Pinterest, the one that had started this particular quest. She looked on the internet every single day. Studied daycare pictures on many different internet sites—those that posted photos with parents' permission. She searched social media sites, too. And any time she saw a child who even halfway resembled the age-progressed photo she had of Jackson, within the distance parameters she'd set, she and Johnny would plan an Angel's Food Bowls trek to the area and visit daycares while they were there. All daycares on her list that also fit the parameters she'd figured Jackson's father would choose, not just those with pictures.

Always on her days off from the hospital. Working three twelves had its advantages.

The police were looking for Jackson, of course. But their jurisdiction was only in Mission Viejo. He was also on the FBI's list of missing children, but apparently no one had the staff to check out every single daycare in every city in California, searching for one missing boy—especially when said child was known to be with his father who'd never given indication of being dangerous. That unfortunate truth, that her case wasn't top priority, had become obvious to her almost from the beginning.

Johnny had very generously insisted on paying for a private detective, who was in contact with the police and would follow up on any leads when the police had done what they could, but it wasn't enough for her. She had to do all *she* could, too. Even if that meant systematically visiting daycare after daycare. Jackson needed her to be out there looking for him. Tuned in the way only a mother could be.

The room just inside the daycare door was painted in primary colors and held plastic chairs and big boxes for sitting on in the same colors. There were some books scattered about and a wire-and-bead maze toy on a little table. A small reception window was cut into the far wall. And, in the middle of that wall, was another heavy wooden door with a dead bolt.

A sign indicated that no one was allowed beyond that door other than certified employees and the children for whom they cared during business hours. For the safety of the children.

She and Johnny would have to return after hours if they wanted a tour. She'd already known that and they wanted a tour.

His hand on her elbow drew her attention, and he pointed to the window where a woman stood, smiling expectantly.

She'd opened the window.

"Ms. Jones?" The woman's shoulder-length brown hair was trimmed stylishly around her slender face. Dressed in a brightly colored tie-dyed short-sleeved shirt, she could've been at a beach fashion shoot. Her name badge, complete with a dotted rendition of a bouncing ball, read *Mallory*.

The owner! Good.

"Yes." Tabitha stepped forward. She'd called to say they were stopping by. To make sure it was okay. "This is Johnny," she said, gesturing at the man beside her.

She was there under false pretenses, but wasn't going to out-and-out lie any more than she had to. And no more than an undercover officer or PI would have done to rescue a little boy from a man who had mental and emotional issues.

Clearly issues that went far, far beyond what she'd known or she'd never have let him take Jackson to visit his sick mother.

"I emailed you about looking at The Bouncing Ball as a possible spot for our daughter?"

She was the one who'd come up with the idea of making their imaginary child a little girl. She needed to do that to keep her emotional distance. Talking about a boy would've been much harder without revealing anything.

Forcing herself to look the woman in the eye, she left it to Johnny to see as much of the inside of the place as he could, not that there was much. According to The Bouncing Ball website, part of the allure was that the privately owned daycare facility took great measures to protect the security of their children. Which was why they'd have to take their tour after hours. But there could be pictures on the wall beyond the receptionist window, maybe. She'd have her chance to check it out, later, if all went well, but she had to do this right.

She had to be ready to see her son without giving herself away or she'd risk looking like an emotionally disturbed woman who might need a restraining order against her. Or something. Johnny had described all the legal pitfalls over and over as they'd started to discuss her desperate idea a month or so after they'd met.

"Yes. She's two, right?" Mallory Harris asked with another smile and a nod as she left the window and came out through the door, handing Tabitha a packet of daycare information. Just a glance showed Tabitha the plethora of material she'd be poring over with Johnny, from permits to payment plans, application guidelines, company policies, schedules…everything. They'd be looking for anything that could help them catch a man who'd probably changed his name—and that of his child.

Through his work at the children's hospital, Mark, Jackson's father, would've known more about birth certificates than a lot of people. He'd had access to medical records. The police thought it most likely that he'd changed Jackson's name and had a fake birth certificate made to support the change.

"Her name's Chrissy," Johnny supplied. They'd named their fake child after an old doll Tabitha had had as a kid; it had been her mother's and it was a doll she still had. You could grow the doll's hair by pushing a button on her belly—a seeming miracle to a very young Tabitha. It was also an effort to keep her mother, who'd been killed in a car accident when Tabitha was in college, a part of the search. Like having a very special angel working with them every step of the way.

"We'd love to take you up on your offer of a tour," Tabitha said now. "We're just stopping in to pick up the materials." She raised the packet she held, afraid she was coming across as a nervous ninny. Jackson could be in this very building. Her precious baby boy…

Johnny's hand lightly touching her spine brought her back to the present task—almost as though he'd known she was having a rougher time this go-round.

"We own a food truck," he said. "We're parked at Mission Beach and plan to close by seven. Would eight o'clock be okay?"

Jackson would be gone by then. But they could find out about any upcoming open houses or recitals or programs The Bouncing Ball might be hosting by checking out posters and signs and leading the conversation casually to that point.

"Eight would be fine. I'm usually here until then, anyway," Mallory said in her easy, open manner. "I get twice the work done when I have the place to myself…"

Tabitha wondered about the woman's family, how they felt about her working six days a week from morning until late at night—and then reminded herself that just because Mallory was there that morning didn't mean she was in early *every* morning. Or even that she worked every day.

Tabitha was surprised by how much she liked Mallory on first meeting. And felt guilty for deceiving her.

It was because this woman might have—please, God—Jackson in her care, Tabitha told herself. Trembling from the inside out, she thanked Mallory Harris, tried to convey with her smile what she couldn't say in words and silently begged Mallory to love her son until she could find a way to get him back.

Chapter Two

Thankful for the food truck that provided frenetic distraction and took a lot of physical and mental energy, Tabitha worked hard beside Johnny all day Monday, barely taking time to nibble on the contents of a bowl with everything. Sitting in the driver's seat as she ate, she watched Johnny take orders and then make the bowls, joking with customers, talking to them from inside the truck as he worked, never missing a beat.

He was drop-dead gorgeous. She'd seen him shirtless on the beach. His baby blues and ready grin didn't hurt, either.

Stepping sideways from the window to his prep board, he grabbed a knife that had cost as much as her monthly car payment and began chopping with expert precision.

You'd think he'd been born a chef rather than the only son of a prominent California family who'd groomed him from birth to take a top legal position within his father's enormous holdings.

The way he played acoustic guitar on the beach, you'd be forgiven for thinking he'd been born to become an entertainer, too.

But Johnny loved to play and sing; he just had no passion for performing. No desire at all to enter the cutthroat world of the music business. No real need for fans or accolades, either.

No need for her accolades…not that she offered them.

A female voice ordered a veggie bowl with extra dressing. Johnny's comment, something about the dressing, made the woman laugh.

Tabitha had grown to crave the laughter he brought to her life. Just as she'd grown to love putting on her light purple polo shirt with the Angel's Food Bowls logo on it and climbing up into his food truck with him. She'd helped him create the logo. And choose the shirts.

His sabbatical was three-quarters through, which meant that in another three months he'd be leaving "normal" life to resume his place in the society of the elite. She had to shudder even thinking about it. To have people watching you all the time, to always be "on," to have to go to extremes, like taking a sabbatical and buying a little house through a third party just to get enough anonymity to grieve… She didn't envy him that.

But she could tell that he missed it all—the life he'd been born to. The way he talked about his parents, his uncle, his cousins. They were a close-knit family.

And *that* she envied.

She was going to miss him terribly when their time together came to an end…

"Eat up there, missy, line's a-forming," he said with a grin in her direction. She blinked. Realized she'd been staring at him. And accidentally toppled her half-filled rice bowl off her lap and onto the floor of the truck.

Never one to cry over spilled milk, as the saying went, Johnny didn't give a rat's ass about the dressing-smeared rice, veggie and meat mixture plastered on the floor near his seat in the hundred-thousand-dollar food truck. He cared that Tabitha was so far off her game he'd hardly recognized her that morning.

She'd been near tears when she'd thanked him for helping in her quest to find Jackson. Her hand had been shaking when she'd passed him a cup of coffee. She hadn't caught several things he'd said to her, although they'd been in the truck together. And she'd messed up two orders.

A pediatric nurse had to be able to keep calm in the midst of horrible stress and, sometimes, unbelievable tragedy. This woman had lost her son and missed less than two weeks of work in the year since.

But that day, stress seemed to be getting the better of her.

Unable to give in to his instant desire to head to the front of the truck and help her clean up the mess, or do it for her, he continued to work the crowd. He prepared a bowl, took off his gloves to make change and then washed his hands, pulling on a fresh set of disposable gloves before preparing the next order.

Then she slid into place in front of the window to accept payment for his most recently completed concoction. That allowed him to keep on his prep gloves, but he couldn't help contaminating them anyway, with a hand to her back. Letting her know she wasn't alone.

"You okay to do this tonight?" The question burst from Johnny about a mile from the daycare just after dark fell that July evening. He'd been trying to figure out a subtler way to ask it for most of the afternoon.

"Of course!" Tabitha's over-the-top enthusiasm—over-the-top for her—brought more concern rather than easing it. From the wheel of the little SUV he'd purchased to tow behind the food truck, he could only afford a quick glance in her direction. But it was enough to tell him, as if he didn't already know, that this trip was different from all the rest.

And that it was taking a toll on her.

He just wasn't sure what he was supposed to do about it. His role seemed to be changing, but they hadn't discussed that. He had no idea *how* it would change, what it would become. They were friends. They talked. Even cried a little.

But they each went home to their own privacy, to dispel the deepest stuff alone.

Their friendship had come with an end date before it had begun. They'd both understood that from the beginning. It was part of why they worked. Why they were able to provide each other with the opportunity they both needed for venting and sharing.

There was no judgment and there were no expectations, nothing to further complicate things. Because they both knew they were living in a time out of time. Both of them had other lives they'd return to as soon as their goals were achieved.

They were helping each other with plans they'd made before they met, not embarking on a life they'd built together.

She'd already collected a list of daycares within her chosen parameters before he'd moved in next to her and had just added to it as time passed—a few of those she'd found had posted pictures that bore a slight resemblance to Jackson. Many did not. All of her daycare searches were within a day's journey by car. According to Tabitha, Mark was obsessive about his mother and wouldn't stray too far from her grave. Over the past six months of working the food truck, Johnny had visited every daycare on

Tabitha's growing list. Starting in Mission Viejo and working outward.

Of course, the daycares that posted actual pictures of their kids were in the minority, and could only do so with parental permission. It wasn't likely that a man who'd kidnapped his son would grant that permission. Still, looking on the internet every night, finding the occasional photo kept her going.

The Bouncing Ball daycare stood out from the rest because it had a client with a Pinterest board she'd created celebrating her own child. And, odd as it was to Johnny, some modern-day parents seemed to think it was cool to plaster pictures of their kids—and even their kids' classmates and pals—all over their social media pages. He got it to a degree; friends and family could all share the special moments.

But so could strangers who preyed on postings like that.

And then there was Tabitha, searching daycare websites and pictures every night. She'd typed in "San Diego daycare" on Pinterest, and seen the picture the mother had posted, along with the name of her toddler's daycare. The parent had probably thought she was doing a good thing, giving the daycare publicity.

Tabitha was completely convinced that the picture she'd seen, the one she'd printed and kept in her purse for at least four days, was of a two-year-old Jackson. Certain. Said she'd seen herself in the eyes gleaming up at the camera. He'd been grinning, along with half a dozen other kids.

"It might not be him." His job was to support, not discourage. But she was in over her head on this one. He could feel it.

"It's him." His peripheral vision told Johnny she was

watching him, but with the traffic, he couldn't take his gaze off the road. Wasn't even sure he wanted to.

"He looked healthy, Johnny. And happy, too…"

Was that why she'd fixated on that particular photo, that particular kid, when there'd been a dozen others during the months they'd been friends? Because the boy had struck her as being happy?

"I understand why now," she continued, sounding like she was giving testimony at a church rather than conversing about her missing son. As if she was somehow seeing some kind of sign. Sacred. Unquestionable.

The whole thing was scaring the hell out of him. For her sake. And his, too, in that he had no idea what to do about any of it.

If she'd been Angel, he'd have asked the tough questions. He'd have pushed. And she'd have told him what was in her deepest heart. Together they'd have figured out a Plan B. Because there was always a chance that Plan A wouldn't work out…

Tabitha's Plan B had always been the next photo. The next daycare. She'd never before indicated that she'd found her end point.

"He's happy because of Mallory Harris… She's, I don't know. I felt confident in her ability to not only watch over the children in her care, but to truly love them. That's why Jackson looked so happy. He's being loved."

Tabitha had once told him she was sure she'd been born to be in the pediatric medical profession. She'd known, even as a young kid playing with her dolls, that she was going to grow up to help sick children.

They hadn't been baring their souls or anything. The topic had come up when he'd been telling her about the reason for his sabbatical. About Angel's passion to own and run her own food truck and his quest to live it for her, since she couldn't. It was a way of preserving her dream, of honoring her life, far more than hanging onto the restaurant she'd owned and run. He'd sold that, used some of the money for the food truck start-up, and donated the rest.

He'd been expecting Tabitha's reaction to it all to be more of the pat on the head his father had given him.

Instead, she'd understood completely. Hadn't just encouraged him, but offered to help in any way she could. Because she had a passion of her own—her yearning to help children in need. Separate and apart from her own immediate and completely pressing determination to find her son.

Leaving him to wonder if he was the only one who didn't seem to have been given that one talent, one thing, that ignited passion within him. Or maybe it was just the passion he lacked.

"And I think it means that Mark is loving him, too," Tabitha's words broke into his thoughts. "As long as Jackson is little, Mark will get what he needs from him," she said as he rounded the last corner and could see the professional building ahead. "Right now, with Jackson completely dependent on him, the whole codependency thing works. But when Jackson starts to assert his own independence—which the terrible twos will certainly bring on…" Her voice drifted off and he was pretty sure she'd just shuddered.

Was that why she was suddenly changing, seeming almost desperate? Not because of this one photo, but because Jackson had turned two and she was getting scared? Worried about her son's safety when he clashed wills against an emotionally unbalanced father?

"Kids learn about their world by challenging their boundaries," she was saying as he pulled into the parking lot. "Of course, Mark's never shown a single violent tendency to me or any of the others who knew him at the hospital. Or, at least, not that any of us ever heard of. There's no reason to assume he'd physically hurt Jackson…but there'd been no reason to suspect he'd kidnap him, either…"

Which could be why the police weren't finding them. Not only were there fewer resources being allocated on a case gone cold, but Mark wasn't a man who raised any alarms, or drew attention. Johnny parked at the daycare but left the engine running. Tabitha's son's father had been a nuclear medicine technician at the children's hospital where she worked. He'd been wonderful with the kids, she'd told him months ago. The guy had quit shortly after Tabitha had broken up with him. His ailing mother had needed full-time care.

He'd still lived with her, apparently, although Tabitha hadn't actually known that until after their breakup.

Those golden eyes with the flecks of green turned on him and Johnny had to draw a long breath. "What's Mark going to do when Jackson challenges their mutual dependency? When Jackson wants independence?" she asked, meeting his gaze head-on. "Taking Jackson makes Mark a criminal, but it doesn't make him violent," he said, drawing on case studies from law school. "A man who made his living helping sick children… I assume he'd have to have a decent bedside manner to keep his job."

She nodded and he continued. "And a guy who nursed his mother so she could die with dignity as she wanted to, at home…"

Tabitha had given him those details months ago. Thankfully he'd remembered enough to be able to repeat them back to her now, when she needed to hear them.

She nodded again. "You're right. He's gentle and nurturing…" She grabbed the handle of her door.

She was ready to go in. His job was done. For another few minutes, at least.

The Bouncing Ball could have been any number of other daycares she and Johnny had toured over the past six months in various southern California cities. Still wearing the jeans and matching purple polo shirts they'd worn all day on the truck, they'd seen the two rooms designated for two-year-olds. They also saw a larger three-year-olds' room, for next year when "Chrissy" was ready to move up. They'd toured the walled-in outdoor playground, accessible only from inside the daycare and outfitted with top-rated equipment, including swings and slides geared for younger children. The lunchroom, was furnished with plastic tables and chairs suited to toddlers.

They'd seen a multipurpose room, complete with a small stage, and heard the sound equipment in use. They'd even been invited to take turns at the musical instruments in a soundproof room intended for early music lessons. While the orchestral instruments were only used by instructors, there was a keyboard, a drum set and a plastic guitar with real strings made for little fingers. And there were various other noisemakers, from maracas to bells and tambourines, that the kids could use with supervision.

From room to room, as she saw the high-quality accommodations, Tabitha couldn't help gushing about how much "Chrissy" would love it there, how happy she, herself, would be as a parent to know that her child was spending her time away from home in such a safe and nurturing place.

Inside she was shaking—with relief, gratitude and fear—as she looked at the surroundings she was certain had housed her baby boy for the past year. Picturing Jackson there, believing that he'd been in this wonderful place, believing that Mark had at least found the best care for their son, brought the relief. The gratitude. Seeing what she supposed her son must have seen for the past year kept her tears close to the surface.

And the thought of being there, possibly tipping Mark off that he was soon to be caught, struck fear in her.

Twice she'd been on the verge of exposing too much of the emotion raging insider her, and both times she'd felt Johnny's hand on the small of her back. Both times he happened to ask Mallory Harris a question pertinent to their tour. Both times she was grateful he was there.

And grateful that they'd be going back to their hotel together that night, to share a glass of wine in the living area of the suite Johnny always insisted on getting for them, before parting to go to their separate rooms. As with all the other tours, he'd sit with her, discuss what they'd seen and heard. He'd ask if she'd felt anything, if her mother's instinct had alerted her to anything. And he'd be supportive. Helping her maintain hope. He was giving her wonderful memories in the midst of the absolute worst time of her life.

No matter how much she'd been craning to look for any sign of Jackson, she saw nothing that night.

Nor had Mallory said anything to indicate that something could be amiss. They had questions they asked on every tour. Carefully worded questions about steps daycare personnel take if they ever see or suspect foul play. How they handle bullying. And how they help children without siblings join in group play. Things that could indicate if they'd had any recent suspicions or experience with foul play, or a toddler with no siblings.

"And over here—" they were finishing the tour with a miniature gymnasium, really only the size of a big bedroom, but complete with gym floor and miniature basketball hoops "—are our trophies," Mallory said, taking them to a plexiglass-enclosed case that resembled something you might see outside a high school auditorium. Johnny moved forward; she knew he was something of a sports buff who'd played varsity baseball and basketball in high school.

Tabitha came up behind him to peer over his shoulder. Simply to be polite, not because she had an extra brain cell to allot to sports awards. She glanced at them, her mind on how to finagle a way to see Jackson. For the first time ever, she'd felt something when they'd walked in. Maybe if they enrolled "Chrissy" they could get a roster of the parents of the other two-year-olds for carpooling or fund-raising activities. Not that a roster would give her Jackson, since Mark had obviously changed their names or the police would already have found them. But she could see if there were any two-year-old boys who had only a father listed.

A little face had been staring back at her from a photo on one side of the case as her mind wandered... and then Tabitha was grabbing Johnny's shoulders, leaning against his back, thinking she might actually be going down.

He turned, his arm sliding around her, and although she was still leaning heavily on him, the dizziness passed as quickly as it had come.

"That photo of the kids who were on the winning team in the Easter egg hunt..."

"As I said, we find ways to get everyone into the

showcase," Mallory said. "We have to be a bit creative with the littles, but at The Bouncing Ball, every single one of our children is a winner."

Mallory's voice faded in and out. Tabitha didn't turn around, didn't look at the photo again. Didn't need to. She had a cropped copy of it in the purse she'd left in the car. It was the photo the mother had posted on the internet of her little girl at school this Easter.

"...not everyone wins all the time," Mallory Harris was saying. "And there are some who think that teaching kids that everyone's a winner is not preparing them for real life. But I believe that every single person on earth has the potential to win at *something*, whether it's at being a parent or being good in a sport, at a job, good at cooking or growing flowers. Or good at smiling and making others feel happy. We all have something special to offer the world, and I like to think that after spending their first four years with us, our kids are better prepared to look for whatever that something special is—in themselves and others."

Tabitha was nodding vigorously. She could feel tears pressing at the backs of her eyes. Jackson's team had won an Easter egg hunt. The picture on the internet had just shown the top halves of the children's bodies, not the entire scene out in the daycare yard.

"That little boy in the front of the photo... He's holding the basket..."

"Jason, yes. He was the team captain and got to carry the basket," Mallory was saying. She didn't give a last name. Didn't reveal any information. But...

Jason. Close to the *Jackson* the one-year-old had known as his name. *Jason.* Now they had a name to offer the police in Mission Viejo, who would get in touch with the San Diego department. She'd learned how it would work if she ever got any information regarding her son's case. Not that she'd told anyone besides Johnny and the investigator he'd hired what she was doing.

The FBI had been called in when Jackson first went missing; they had a special team that had been particularly helpful during the critical first hours—but local police had also stayed involved.

Jackson was still on file as a missing person, but law enforcement had seen many other cases come and go since his disappearance. There was only so much they could do without more to go on. There'd been virtually no new leads.

Until she'd found one.

Jason.

"His parents must've been really proud of him," she said, still leaning on Johnny although most of her strength had returned, for the moment, anyway, as she addressed the other woman.

"His dad was," Mallory said casually as she led them back to the daycare's entry. "Jason's mom passed away, died of liver disease a year after his birth."

Jason's dad had been a single father for the past year. Jackson had been stolen away from her by his father a year ago. Jason's mother had supposedly died a year after his birth. Jackson had been stolen from her a year after his birth.

Johnny held her up. They were at the door and she couldn't make her feet move to get her out of there. Jason's supposed mother had died of liver disease the year before. Mark's mother had died of liver disease a year ago. It was something he'd be able to talk about in detail, having nursed her to the end of her life. That would have given credibility to his lies.

Jason was Jackson. She'd *known*. She'd hoped she was right. She'd thought she was.

Now she *knew* she'd known.

After twelve long, excruciating months, she'd found her son.

Chapter Three

Johnny understood life, particularly his role in it. He worked hard enough to be the best at whatever he did. He took satisfaction from that. He did what was expected of him, expected by himself and others. He went with the flow.

Strong urges, other than the normal sexual ones a guy got, didn't play a significant role in his life. He wasn't driven. Had no great passion. He was a mind guy all the way.

Which was why that Monday night in July, the evening of his daycare visit with Tabitha, would remain with him forever. He didn't understand why he couldn't walk away from her—the steps it would take to get him to his room in their suite. His mind told him to leave. Something unfamiliar held him rooted to the spot.

"Go have your shower," he told her. "I'll order some dinner and open a bottle of wine." They'd picked up a couple of bottles down by the beach the evening before from a shop selling local wines. They'd bought a limited-production white that had won an award at San Diego's Toast of the Coast Wine Competition.

They'd talked about having a glass. He'd been thinking about it on and off all day. A glass of wine with Tabitha. But she'd been quiet on the ride back from the daycare. The kind of quiet that meant she needed some time alone. Some space.

Usually they talked after a visit, but when she got quiet like that, he was supposed to leave her alone in her world, knowing she'd be back when she was ready.

He was supposed to go to his room.

That was their way, and it had been established from the very beginning—by deed more than conversation—and neither of them had ever deviated from it.

So what the hell was he doing? More crucially, *why*?

It wasn't the first time she'd thought she found her son. He was quite certain it wouldn't be the last. He only wished he was as certain that she *would* find the child someday. And that this boy, Jason, was her Jackson...

He'd rinsed off quickly, dressed in a newish pair of tan shorts and a black polo shirt, and was pouring the wine by the time Tabitha's bedroom door opened. He hadn't been sure she'd come back out.

She'd put on the tie-dyed, spaghetti-strap, calf-length sun dress she wore at home a lot on her days off. It had reds and browns in it, offset by gold. The casual red Italian sandals she wore with it struck him as odd, since they weren't going anywhere. He was barefoot. Just as he always was around the house these days.

He kept looking at the curves of her calves, finding them erotically attractive—calves. Tabitha's calves.

One look at her face, though, and erotic thoughts fled. This was *Tabitha*. And the unfamiliar light in her eyes, as though she was bursting with secrets and ready to fly off her rocker in some kind of desperation, or so his imagination told him, called to him in an entirely different way.

He handed her a glass of wine. Held his up and waited for her to tip hers to it, as they always did.

"To our goals," he said. She clinked her glass against his, but didn't repeat the toast. She sipped instead. Then she curled up on the sofa, her feet tucked into that cute butt.

He sat on the other end of the couch, glass in hand.

"It's him, Johnny."

She sounded…different then she had before. The whole desperation thing?

Again, what did he do with that!? His job was to encourage her, to keep her spirits up so they didn't pull her permanently under. To let her know she wasn't alone.

And to be Chrissy's dad sometimes.

Hers was to help him make a success of Angel's food truck.

He had another three months of sabbatical. There was no reason for her to panic, yet. To think her time was running out.

"A lot can happen in three months," he said.

Her nod was a relief. Until she said, "We need a plan, though. Time's not the issue. Neither is the truck, since we're doing better than either of us imagined and sold more here in one day than we have anywhere else. We can come down every week on my days off. It'll save having to get permits in other counties, finding new spots… You'll be able to build a real following."

The food truck was his last concern at the moment. But he liked the practical way her mind was working, so he nodded. "Fine with me."

Her smile warmed him as he took his next sip, and he told himself it was really the wine that had affected him. But he wasn't exactly buying the explanation. Two days in a row now, he'd been getting the hots for Tabitha.

Stranger things had happened than a perfectly healthy guy being attracted to an absolutely gorgeous woman. Except that he'd been traveling with her, living next door to her, sharing dinners and suites with her, for months without thinking about taking her to bed.

"We need a plan," she said again, her expression needy, confident and expectant all at the same time.

A plan for sleeping together and remaining friends until their exit date? He'd set aside a year of his life to honor Angel. He couldn't sleep with another woman.

Trashing his first "plan" thought, he took a moment to come up with another.

Tabitha had been different ever since she'd seen that online picture of the boy at The Bouncing Ball the previous week. She'd run over to his house, coming in without knocking—which they did when they were expecting each other. But this time there'd been no warning. He could've been standing in the kitchen naked instead of in his pajama bottoms…

He might have said something, too, if he hadn't noticed the tears in her eyes, the trembling of her hands as she held out the picture she'd just printed.

Yeah, she'd been different ever since.

And so had he.

This whole thing of his…it was her fault. Her barging in on him in his pajamas.

"What kind of plan?" he finally asked when nothing useful was forthcoming.

"Detective Bentley won't be able to compel a DNA test based on what we've got. We need to find a way to get more. Alistair can follow up on the name Jason, but without a last name…"

Alistair Montgomery was the PI Johnny had hired. The guy was willing to do whatever Johnny asked as long as he got paid for it. But following up on a common first name? In San Diego?

Not liking where this was going, he felt everything slow down as he watched her. "What exactly have we got?"

"Jason—Jackson. Single dad. A year. Liver disease. A picture that matches the age-progression photo."

She listed everything as though going over facts that were a given, as though hoping they'd see what might be missing. He wondered how long it would be before she figured out *he* was missing from this collection of hers. Or rather, his buy-in… The picture might closely resemble the age-progression, but he wouldn't call it a match.

"Liver disease?"

"Mark's mother died of it," she said, and he remembered her having told him that. After he'd first met her and she'd been telling him her story. That last visit, Mark's mother had just died, but she hadn't known that when she dropped Jackson off at the home Mark shared with his mother. They passed off in the driveway…

He nodded. "That's right…" He drew the word out, as if he was getting it now, while frantically trying to figure out how to support her, be a friend, encourage her, without lying.

"So, any ideas?"

He wanted to empty his glass in one long gulp. He held on to it, instead, saying nothing.

"Come on, Johnny, you're always the one with the plans. What can we do, legally? What rights do I have?"

She was serious. Stone-cold, go-to-your-grave serious.

Brain in full gear, he ran the facts through his mind. A little boy, Jason. A missing one, the same age, with a similar name, Jackson. One appearing in San Diego about the time the other disappeared from Mission Viejo.

Single dads. A mother and a wife dying from the same disease at the same time.

It was enough to give false hope to a desperate woman—he could see that. But it was circumstantial at best. And not even enough of that to compel law enforcement to do anything.

"I admit that there are similarities." He started slowly. He couldn't dash her hopes. Not because of any role he was playing in her life, but because…he just couldn't. This was Tabitha. And he couldn't do that to her. Even with cause.

"It's him, Johnny, I'm sure of it."

He wanted to believe her in the worst way.

Tried. But couldn't.

Still, what did he know about mother's instinct and such? Or any pull from the gut that was nonsexual in nature?

He loved his folks. Had loved Angel, too, although his feelings for her had been more of a warm fondness than any great passion. They'd grown up in the same circle. They'd probably gravitated to each other because they were the only ones in their group of rich kids at their private school who hadn't had siblings. Or divorced parents. Or both. Their parents had always thrown them together, wanting them to marry. She'd made no secret of the fact that she was deeply in love with him. And he'd truly loved her, although he just didn't seem to be the type of guy who got passionate about anything.

Hence, his quest to see Angel's passion through.

In any case, he'd loved her. Still loved her. But his feelings were just…there.

There wasn't the kind of bone-deep need in them that Tabitha clearly felt for her son. He'd never felt that way about anyone, in any situation. He'd probably understand it better when he had a child of his own, but until then…

"We have to figure out a way to get DNA samples," Tabitha was saying, sipping wine with more passion than usual.

"Unless Jason's father gives consent, you'd need a warrant," he stated the legal facts. And if Jason's father was Tabitha's Mark, the chances of him giving consent were nil.

But…what would it hurt to help her try to get the sample? Let the science tell her the boy wasn't hers?

The more he thought about it, the more he liked the idea. They'd buy some time. He'd be able to help her one hundred percent. And someone else could be the bearer of bad news—at which point, she'd still have his support and they'd keep looking.

"Do you think we should ask to speak with Jason's father, then? That we should just ask Mark, or whatever he's calling himself these days, to prove that Jason isn't Jackson?"

He didn't immediately respond to her question. If he went along with this, helped her as though he believed, maybe he could prepare her for the possibility that the test, once they found a way to compel it, could come back negative.

Yes. He liked this idea. It was a good one.

With that thought, he drank some of his wine. He could delve into the legal problem at hand. Be a partner to Tabitha again.

"That's not a good idea," he finally replied. "We don't want to force his hand and have him run off again."

"I know. But now that we've found him, maybe if we just confront him…"

He looked her straight in the eye. "Do you think he's

going to give up his son at this point and let himself be carted off to jail?"

She held his gaze for a moment. Long enough to make him feel good all over. To forget, for just a second, what they were doing there. And then she said, "No, of course not."

He nodded. "So we need to keep being Chrissy's parents, keep our undercover identities, and see if there's any more we can find out. We need something compelling enough that when we go to the police, they can do more than just question Mark…which would only tell him it's time to run again—which is why I think we need to stay physically away from the daycare. If that boy is Jackson, you don't want Mark to come walking in and find you there. What we need is to somehow get enough of a lead to help Alistair. A last name would be a great place to start. He could look into this Jason's father."

She nodded, then took a sip of her own wine. In his opinion, the wine was excellent. She seemed to think so, too. He stood up to get the bottle to top off both their glasses.

"You don't think we should go to the police yet? Call Detective Bentley? Or have someone here in San Diego at least do a wellness check on Jason?"

Her pleading glance made him sit closer to her as he shook his head and rejoined her on the couch.

"First of all, Mallory—whom you obviously trust—didn't give the slightest hint that there's anything wrong. Unless there's some reason to suspect something's wrong, more than we currently have on Jason, they won't be able to do any more than tell him someone asked for a wellness check. They'd more than likely see that he's well."

"Couldn't we have them ask him for a DNA sample, just to settle this?"

"If they'd even agree to do that, which is highly unlikely with only circumstantial evidence, I can almost guarantee you his answer would be an unequivocal no. And then, if it *is* Mark, he'll definitely be tipped off."

"Wouldn't that be like an admission of guilt?"

"You'd think so, but no. People guard their privacy, especially these days. But what it *could* do is make Mark nervous…"

"…and that we don't want. Not while he still has Jackson. Not only because he could run again, but because we have no idea if…"

The stark fear in her gaze burned a hole so deep in him, he felt places he hadn't known existed. "You've said all along that he's gentle and kind. Patient. Great with kids," he quickly reminded her. He didn't know whether a man who was unhinged enough to kidnap his son because his own mother had died would be capable of hurting the boy. He just knew that Tabitha's clutching that fear served no good purpose.

"He is." She nodded once again, her smile filled with the kind of thanks a man wanted to hold on to.

He wanted to hold on to *her.* To pull her into his arms and keep her there. For a little while, anyway. Then he'd let her go. Before violating their friendship, making things messy, which would lead to an earlier end to their relationship than planned.

He didn't want that.

Tabitha wasn't anything like the other women in his world—and had absolutely no interest in becoming one of them—a woman who lived in the society he'd been born to. And he couldn't see himself as anyone other than Johnny Brubaker, top legal counsel for his father's holdings until the old man retired, if he ever retired, at which point the holdings would belong to Johnny. It had all been loosely mapped out before his birth.

"I think what we need to do first is fill out that application and see if we can get Chrissy enrolled at The Bouncing Ball." Legal pitfalls bounced all around him. Over him.

"Don't we need a two-year-old girl to do that?"

"She's not the one who'll be looked at. We will be." He'd already perused the application. It was general stuff. Their jobs. Addresses. "We can use your home address and then the address of the commissary I rented here for the week…" Food truck laws in California required a street address for the business, one that passed health code regulations for storing and preparing food, and included a place where the truck could be parked. "I'll rent it for the rest of the month. We can explain that we're moving here and that Chrissy's at home with… my mother."

For the first time that day, Tabitha's features relaxed. She looked like herself. Because they had a plan.

He thought about his mother…and Tabitha…and started to squirm inside again.

Tabitha knew his family had money, that he and Angel had gone to private school with limousine transportation to and from. She knew he'd been legal counsel for his father's business. She didn't know how rich they were and that he'd been groomed to be lead counsel for a team of about twenty. And his parents had no idea how or where he was currently living. There was no way he was inviting them to the little place he'd bought. They'd worry about him more than they already were. They'd agreed to give him his year to grieve Angel, to leave him alone as long as he called regularly.

And he couldn't very well just show up at the mansion with Tabitha, unless he gave her some kind of heads-up.

It wasn't like his family owned a business that she could just look up on the internet and learn all about them. More like, his father invested in many diverse interests, from patents to oil rigs, but only with his own capital. He wasn't an investor for others. Sometimes he invested in failing companies and brought them around. It was always about the next challenge to him. Just as it had been for his father before him.

"I don't know how to thank you, Johnny," she said, "But if you need me to wash your clothes for you for the rest of your sabbatical, I'm game." Her grin was like a hundred others she'd given him over the months and the world righted itself.

Then he caught a glimpse of a random drop of moisture on her top lip. He couldn't look away. And knew he'd pay a high price for what that minute drop of wine made him want to do.

Chapter Four

Tabitha stared at Johnny's bare feet. He had nice feet. Toes aligned. Tanned. Nothing knobby about them. Good enough to be a foot model, if he'd been so inclined. She'd told him so once.

He'd quirked his eyebrow at her and continued whatever conversation they'd been having at the time.

"Did you go barefoot a lot growing up?" she asked now, still thinking about him saying they'd say that "Chrissy" was with his mother as they sat together on the couch in their suite sipping wine. She understood why she hadn't met his family, but that didn't mean she didn't wonder about them.

Other than this year away, his entire life revolved around them. He worked for the family. Had married his parents' best friends' daughter. Lived close enough to them that he'd made it to his own bed with his own two feet after getting blistering drunk in his father's den, with his father, on the night of his wife's funeral. He had more aunts, uncles and cousins than she had acquaintances. And he was an only child.

She didn't know that man. But as their time together

grew shorter, she *wanted* to know him. Felt she needed to know him.

She was ready to recover her son. She wasn't anywhere near ready to lose the friend she'd found in Johnny. Wasn't sure she'd ever be ready for that.

And yet she realized she had to be. She was a loner. Other than her small circle, anonymity was her comfort.

He hadn't answered her question. He was watching her, though. Probably wondering why she was talking about feet when they'd been discussing their plan to get Jackson back.

"I like it that you go barefoot," she told him, needing to have a moment of non-Jackson conversation. To breathe. "You're so…smart. And together. It's not surprising that everything you touch turns to gold. You have life so figured out, it actually works the way it's supposed to—well other than Angel, of course…" She paused, and then added, "But your whole life has been a plan…and yet your feet…they're free. You've got things together enough to leave room for freedom."

If there'd ever been babbling, that was it. Award-winning wine was potent.

"I'd never gone barefoot in my life, other than at the beach, the pool or in the shower, until I moved next door to you."

Wait. Was he saying he was barefoot because of something *she'd* done? That she'd released something inside him?

Impossible! But…maybe?

The way he was looking at her…he seemed to need her to understand something important. And she wanted to. For months she'd been wanting to. Their time together was going to be gone soon and she didn't know him well enough.

Didn't know what he felt when he got all quiet on her.

Didn't know how he really felt about her. Other than as the other participant in their time out of real life to reach their goals.

"It started with your sabbatical?" she asked. "Going barefoot, I mean."

"The carpet in the house is white," he reminded her.

Cream-colored, but…yes. And the soles of his shoes would mark it in a day. So practical. So…Johnny. Maybe she knew him better than she thought.

"So our plan is to put in an application at The Bouncing Ball to gain access to more information in the hope of finding something that will link Jason and his father to Mark and Jackson?" she asked, her mind back on track. "We can enroll over the internet, so we don't have to go back where Mark might see us, and maybe get a parent list? At the very least we need Jason's last name."

They needed to stay on track. It was just so hard, being alone in the world except for her coworkers, who'd once been closer friends than they were now. She'd shut them out to focus fully on her search for Jackson. Losing her son made her feel so powerless. So helpless.

"That's the plan," Johnny said, willing, as always, to let go of any moment that might verge on discomfort.

With her, anyway. In his real life he was a high-powered corporate attorney.

A man she didn't know.

Setting down her glass of wine, Tabitha thanked him for being the best friend she'd ever had and said goodnight.

She wanted to stay. To ask him tough questions. Real questions. To touch his heart, let him know how much he'd touched hers.

To ask if there was any way he'd be willing to consider a longer-term agreement.

His easy smile followed her across the room as he lifted the bottle they'd been sharing and poured himself a little more wine.

With the half wave that was her usual "see ya," Tabitha closed her bedroom door, buried her face in her pillow and cried herself to sleep.

In fresh jeans and a clean purple *Angel* shirt, Tabitha brought along a fresh state of mind as she worked beside Johnny the next morning in the prep kitchen he'd rented for the next month.

He grilled the pork and steak while she seasoned and cooked all the beans. Everything would be refrigerated, then reheated as needed throughout the day.

"I don't think we should cut back on the beans," she told him. "We almost ran out yesterday." Their weekly plan—a spreadsheet he always provided that was taped to a cupboard between them—indicated one gallon can less of each. He'd based that on foot traffic research he'd done on the beach area, which he'd averaged for Tuesdays.

What she wanted to tell him was that she had an idea for a new plan. She'd thought she'd do it on the drive over that morning, but he'd been hell-bent on a particular cup of coffee from a particular place—his favorite—and she'd figured he deserved a morning when coffee was the most important thing on his mind.

Lord knew, between the two of them and their individual needs, those kinds of mornings were few. At least, when they were together. What he did when they weren't working she couldn't say.

Because she didn't ask.

"We should still cut back," he said. He stopped what

he was doing to send her a warm smile, as if to soften the blow of his refusal to accept her opinion on the needed quantity of beans. Johnny almost never paused when he was chopping. Especially beef. Seeming to remember that, he glanced at the knife in his hand and returned his attention to the board on the counter in front of him. "It's Tuesday," he said, by way of explanation.

In the six months they'd been actually out food trucking, as opposed to getting things set up, he'd run out of food exactly twice. So she went along with one fewer can of beans.

"I think instead of applying for Chrissy, we should tell Mallory Harris the truth." That wasn't quite how she'd planned to present her idea, but there it was.

She didn't look at Johnny as she added the bag of his premixed spices to the pan of black beans, adjusting the heat underneath them as she stirred. She listened to him chop, thankful for the even, rhythmic beat of blade against board.

"You're the one who always wants to do things on the up-and-up, to cross all the t's and dot all the i's. And finally having found Jackson, I don't want to do anything that might make me seem less than…"

She barely registered his lack of chopping before she felt his hands on her arms. "It's okay, Tabitha." His easy tone settled the tension building inside her while his hands distracted her from the reason for that tension.

Johnny's touch…it always did that to her. Distracted her. And reassured her.

"You don't have to sound so defensive or feel like you need to convince me. Finding Jackson—how we do it, that's your call."

It was part of their agreement. He called the food truck shots. She called her own.

And suddenly she didn't want to. Not without his input. Not now that they'd found Jackson. Her son was so close, yet not really within her reach.

"I want to tell her," she said again. "She seems to truly care. The way she talked about her hours, working late at night after everyone leaves, and if she's there during the day, which by what she said she is… I get the feeling that The Bouncing Ball is way more than a business to her."

"Again, I'm not arguing." He'd moved back to his board but wasn't chopping. They had a prep time limit, one he was going to miss if he didn't get going. Which could mean they'd lose their prime parking spot.

"I think she'll help us," Tabitha said, a spoon in each hand as she stirred both pans of beans. It had only taken her a week to get her prep responsibilities down to a science. When she glanced at him, he quickly looked from her to his board.

He'd been watching her.

"What?" she asked, watching him now. Stirring beans didn't require constant vigilance like wielding the knife did.

He shrugged and she suddenly wondered what those shoulders looked like in a suit coat. Probably not as good as they did in the tight-fitting polo shirt. They'd be as strong, though. As supportive.

"Tell me what you're thinking. Please. I'm asking because I need to know." About Jackson. And the next move in her quest.

"Mallory's first loyalty will likely be to Jason's father. She clearly had sympathy for him and appears to hold him in high regard."

"You're basing that on what?" she asked. The side of his clean-shaven face told her very little, except that he wasn't smiling.

"The warmth in her voice as she mentioned him, for one."

"You think she has a thing for him?" She hadn't gotten that impression at all.

"No. She just seemed…fond of them as clients and might try to protect them."

"You think she'll tell him?"

"I think it's a possibility you should consider."

"And by the time I convince her I'm right, Mark will be gone…with Jackson."

She knew what his shrug meant that time.

"I see the risk, I just wish we could tell her." She turned back to the beans.

"Then let's find something convincing enough to allow us to do that."

Tabitha's heart gave a lurch at the supportive tone in his voice. She looked at him, needing him more than ever. Needing him to know that.

And to need her, too.

He was busy chopping meat.

Like Tabitha, Johnny didn't feel good about putting in Chrissy's application. Tabitha had spent her fifteen-minute break going over the forms she'd filled out sometime between leaving him the night before and them leaving that morning because they'd been waiting for her down at the front desk where she'd emailed them for printing. Forms she'd filled out, even though she'd wanted to forego the Chrissy route and tell Mallory Harris the truth.

Hoping to enlist the daycare owner's help.

Ethically and legally, helping them out could be a disaster for the Harris woman. Unless she had a lawyer watching her every move, protecting her against misadventure.

Tabitha reached above his head for a package of napkins early Tuesday evening, putting her breasts directly in his line of vision. Close enough that if he leaned forward and moved to the side, he could touch one with his lips.

Instantly engorged, Johnny moved, all right, directly forward, tucking the bulging evidence of his inappropriate erection under the prep board.

What the hell! She'd been reaching for napkins for months. In the same purple shirts.

So what was this about? Boredom with the task at hand? He'd never been passionate about the food truck business, but he'd been determined to see Angel's dream through to fruition. He owed her that.

"I think we should hold off on Chrissy's application," he blurted, spraying and wiping the prep board. Tabitha, now back at the closed serving window, filled the napkin dispenser she'd set on the ledge for when they opened the next day.

He'd been reviewing her idea to tell Mallory Harris the truth and actually given it serious consideration. The kind he'd give if he was at work, doing the job he'd been trained to do.

A distraction from getting the hots for his life-quest partner?

For whatever reason, this time, this place, this daycare, seemed different from all the rest. Tabitha felt strongly enough about engaging the Harris woman's help, being honest with her from the beginning, that she'd asked him for advice. Thoughtful, professional advice.

He really wanted to provide it.

A pile of napkins in hand, she held them above the open dispenser, watching him.

"What?" he asked. The concern creasing her brow, shadowing those golden-green eyes, struck his gut.

"You don't want to apply with me?"

Had he said that? And why did kissing those lips seem like such a good move at the moment? It was wrong.

All wrong.

Pulling himself back to their current conversation, he said, "I think I've come up with a way to tell Mallory Harris the truth."

Her brow cleared. Good.

"You think we can get her to help us rather than telling Mark we're here?"

He nodded.

You don't want to apply with me?

He hadn't skipped past those words as easily as she had.

Finished with the napkins, she closed the dispenser and turned to him, eyes wide open. "Okay, so what's the plan?"

You don't want to apply with me?

"Why would you think I don't want to apply with you?"

A direct, personal question. She should turn away. Or he should. She held his gaze. So he held hers, too. Waiting to see what would happen.

"It's…a step we've never had to take before," she said, her voice more hesitant than he was used to. Did the fact that he liked hearing more than her surface tone make him some kind of jerk?

"But it's always been part of the plan," he started. What had changed? Was he sending out bad vibes? Did she somehow sense that he was lusting after her, all of a sudden?

"Talking and doing are different sometimes," she said,

giving him her full attention. It would be rude of him to spray and wipe.

"We're putting lies down on paper," she continued. "And I know how you are about paper trails. If it's written down, you want it to be accurate enough to stand up in court."

He couldn't help the grin that broke out on his face, feeling like he'd dodged a bullet.

"The application itself wouldn't get us into trouble," he told her. "Presenting an actual child under false pretenses, or taking part in daycare activities with other children under false pretenses, that could do it. But the information we put down here, on this initial application, isn't about our imaginary Chrissy. It's about us, and as far as it goes, it's accurate. It says we run a food truck. We do. It gives the kitchen as a contact address, for the next month, it is. It doesn't say you're not a nurse, or I'm not a lawyer, it just doesn't say we are. And, for now, this week, we're a couple. We don't put on here that we're married. Your reference, your friend at the hospital, is legitimate, and my reference is, too."

She nodded. "They might call your parents…"

He was ahead of her. "I called them myself and warned them that if they got any calls to please cooperate."

"You told them about me?" Her question ended on a high note. As if she was shocked.

But glad?

"No. I just told them I was involved with helping out a family…"

She nodded. Disappointed? Relieved?

Did it matter?

"It just felt…like I was doing you a disservice, naming you as the father of my child."

He grew hard again. He felt like a creep as he stayed close to the prep board.

"Your imaginary child," he reminded them both. And then, for reasons completely unknown to him, said, "But being the father of your child would be an honor..."

What?

"For any man worth his salt," he quickly added.

She studied him for a second while he held his breath and thought about checking himself in to some mental facility. Then she smiled. A perfectly normal Tabitha-and-Johnny-life-quest-partners smile.

"But we can look at all the options—including an honest conversation with Mallory."

Her huge smile made him feel as if he'd survived a game of Russian roulette.

Chapter Five

Feeling closer to Johnny than she'd ever felt before, Tabitha stood outside the food truck, watching him lock it up for the night. His back was to her, so his shoulders were there for the staring, and stare she did. By what streak of luck he'd moved in next door to her, she didn't know, but she'd never cease being grateful for his presence in her life.

She'd asked again about his plan to talk to Mallory. He'd suggested they discuss it over dinner. For the moment, her world felt right.

Not happy—not without Jackson—but…close.

Because Jackson wasn't far away. But also because of Johnny.

"I thought maybe we could get some dinner at one of the restaurants on the beach," he told her. "We can find someplace with a patio. It's warm enough to eat outside."

As usual with his suggestions, she was game. And wasn't surprised when it took him less than twenty minutes to find the perfect spot not far from their hotel. He suggested they park at the hotel and walk to dinner, and that sounded great to her, too.

Still dressed in their jeans and Angel's Food Bowl

shirts, they fit right in with the casual crowd as they took their seats on a beach-level patio a short distance from the ocean.

Though the barbeque place drew mostly families, the patio seemed to attract couples. Leaning into each other. Holding hands. The two women on the left doing both as they lifted their wineglasses in a toast.

Maybe newly married?

Focusing her attention on the menu she'd pulled from between the cowboy-boot-shaped salt and pepper shakers, Tabitha tried not to think about how she and Johnny might appear to the other diners around them—if any of them even noticed.

Or to the waitress who stopped by for their drink orders and wasn't the least bit flirtatious, in spite of how inarguably gorgeous Johnny was. As though she respected that he was Tabitha's man.

"You want to share a pitcher of beer?" he asked her, and she nodded—while she flushed at the idea of Johnny as *her* man.

Would she ever marry? She'd always thought so. Especially after her mother had died, leaving her virtually alone in the world. But now...

With Jackson...

She'd been raised by a single parent. Her father had died in Desert Storm before having a chance to marry her mother. Her grandmother, too, had been widowed young.

Maybe it was a thing in their family, a history that bred strong women who stood alone. That could explain why she'd felt so cramped when Mark had gotten so needy. So possessive. He'd have married her in a heartbeat. And her heart just hadn't beat faster for him.

Putting down the menu he'd been studying, Johnny dropped his hands on top of it and looked at her.

"What are you having?"

The question was familiar. Casual. Asked dozens of other times, in other eateries, as they'd traveled around the southern half of the state. No reason for it to seem so...intimate now.

Or to start caring about how they appeared to others.

He'd told his parents he was helping a family.

Which she and Jackson were. A family.

So why had she hoped, for a second there, that he'd mentioned her, in particular?

His parents' good opinion wasn't anything she'd craved, certainly not before now. She'd love to meet them, but only to know Johnny better, because they were such a huge part of his life.

And maybe she wanted them to like her for the same reason.

While she continued to stare at her menu, he was still waiting for her dinner choice.

She knew better than to think she could be part of his life forever. She didn't even want to be. Not the life he was going to return to.

If she hoped now and then, or imagined what it would be like if he opted to stay in his little house rather than move back to wherever he really lived, that was strictly her own business. A fantasy she quickly turned away from.

She'd looked him up on the internet once. There hadn't been much about him, not that she'd found at a glance, but she'd seen that his father was powerful enough to be lunching with senators.

"Did you decide?" When his question came again, she realized she hadn't answered him yet.

"I know you aren't dating during your sabbatical," she

said when she looked up at him, although she'd meant to say, "Steak salad."

He nodded. "That's right," he said. "Doesn't seem like I'd be honoring my wife if I started a relationship with someone else."

She leaned toward him, then realized how that might look. Still, she didn't want to be overheard. He glanced out toward the ocean, brought his gaze back to her and then sat back, an easy smile on his face. "You can't decide what you want to eat?"

"Steak salad," she told him, dismissing the comment she'd been about to share with him. It was their way. If one backed off, the other followed.

It was how they worked.

"Why did you mention my lack of dating?" He still held his relaxed pose, but his gaze was kind of intense. "You interested in someone?" He grinned then. A grin of sorts. "Because, you know, if I'm getting in your way or…"

"No! Oh, my gosh, Johnny, no!" Her hand was on his arm where it lay on the table. "Sorry," she said, pulling back. "I didn't mean to be so loud."

He scanned the patio, seemingly unconcerned, and their waitress returned with their pitcher of beer and two iced glasses. Johnny poured expertly, giving her a filled mug with almost no head. He ordered for both of them. He knew what kind of dressing she wanted on her salad and knew to ask them to leave out the peppers. She liked that.

Too much.

This whole being-close-to-Jackson thing while not being able to just go and get him was making her nuts. The way she'd overreacted when he'd said they should hold off on putting in Chrissy's application. She'd jumped to the crazy conclusion that he was done with her and…

She was messing up her relationship with Johnny and that was the last thing she wanted.

She took a deep breath. "I mentioned your need not to date as part of your sabbatical because I wondered if it bothered you to have people look at us and think we're a couple. Other than at the daycares, of course, we both knew going in that would be a factor. But Kent at the rental office this morning, he obviously thought so. And people here, probably everywhere we go out to eat, in the hotels we stay at…"

"We get two-bedroom suites," he reminded her. "Hardly what a couple would do."

Right. At least, not a couple with him as one half.

Tabitha reached for her beer, visualizing the photograph in her purse. The smile on her two-year-old son's face as he held a basket of plastic eggs. She wanted to rest her head on Johnny's shoulder, feel his arms around her—but that wasn't doing anything except making her weak.

Yeah, thinking of Jackson was hard. Emotions were pushing at her in a way they hadn't done in months. Refusing to be pushed back. What if Mark caught wind that they'd found him and Jackson? What if she got this close and he ran again?

She couldn't afford to make a mistake.

When her thoughts led right back to the point of panic, making the cold sweats and tremors start, she glanced over at Johnny. Saw him watching her.

She smiled at him. He smiled back.

And she wanted to be in his arms.

"So give me your plan for telling Mallory," she said.

Johnny took a sip of beer before he answered Tabitha,

ashamed that her son, her quest, had been the last thing on his mind as he'd been watching her.

Her pain, her beauty, his sudden need to be man to her woman—those thoughts had pretty much occupied his mind. Not necessarily in that order. She'd mentioned dating and his brain had slipped into his pants.

Taking with it all the thoughts and feelings, the scents and memories, of Tabitha Jones.

It occurred to him that she could be feeling it, too, this suddenly intense attraction. It was entirely possible, plausible even, that he felt so off-center because nuances in their relationship were changing.

Like the fact that she'd brought up the subject of dating.

Or worrying that he was going to back out on their life-quest bargain by not being willing to play the part of Chrissy's dad, if necessary.

Asking if he'd mentioned her to his parents…

If he hadn't decided his food truck venture required celibacy while he honored his deceased wife, he might have considered asking Tabitha how she felt about adjusting their bargain to include some physical benefits.

And in doing that, he could ruin a great friendship. In truth, now that he'd had six months on the truck, he didn't see how he could have fulfilled Angel's dream without Tabitha there helping him.

He could always have hired someone, but would that person have also been able to give him the impetus to get the job done as well as Angel deserved? He'd work the truck with or without Tabitha, because that was who he was, but her presence and the promise he'd made her changed things.

She brought out something in him he hadn't seen coming. But he could see it now. He got out of bed in the morning these days because he was eager for the day ahead, not just because the alarm went off.

He'd never answered her question about his plan concerning the daycare. She was people watching, as though she found the other diners fascinating.

"If we're going to tell Mallory Harris the truth, I think we should do it in an appointment scheduled for that purpose, not as an afterthought to what she believes is a meeting regarding Chrissy," he said.

"And we can't do this over the phone," Tabitha jumped in before he could take a breath "We'll have a better chance of getting her to believe that Jason's father kidnapped him if we speak face-to-face. I can show her the age-progressed photo. Plus his baby pictures and all the ones taken during his first year. We can show her the photo of Mark the police had, but as both Detective Bentley and Alistair told us, it's a pretty clear bet that he's altered his appearance. Still, I can tell her about little things Jackson did, like the way he used to do a closed-mouth spit whenever I tried to give him peas…"

Johnny listened because she enthralled him. But when she paused, he continued.

"We'll get to all of that," he said, not in the least surprised that her idea had real substance. She wouldn't have proposed it otherwise. "To arrange that meeting, I suggest we tell her I'm a lawyer. That I'm helping you."

He waited, and when she didn't interject, continued. "We can ask her to meet with us to discuss the details of a situation that's relevant to our earlier visit."

"Chrissy?"

"We'll let her know up-front our interest has to do with her business, but that we aren't comfortable with further discussion unless we can meet face-to-face. I would also emphasize our need for complete confidentiality, but we can't force her to keep quiet. That's the risk we take."

Her brow furrowed. She nodded. "Do you feel it's a worthwhile risk?"

"I do." Because he'd been thinking about it all afternoon and, after considering every aspect through the eyes of the law, he saw that her plan was their best option. With his last caveat. "I'm going to give Alistair a copy of the picture you have from the daycare and ask him to keep an eye on The Bouncing Ball parking lot, looking for a single man with a child who resembles Jackson in the age-progressed photograph."

Her eyes opened wide. "That could mean a couple of hours of surveillance a day, Johnny. I can't ask you to pay out that much." And then, "I don't have a ton of cash, but I've got some. And a huge limit on my credit card that I can use for a cash advance. I can also get a line of credit on my house."

"I intend to pay for it myself," he said. "Since it was my idea…" And since he could easily afford it and he knew she couldn't.

The quick shake of her head had him reaching deeper.

"I'm going to be acting as your lawyer, Tabitha. It's within my realm to do this. I can use it as a tax write-off. And, if you'd like, I can always bill you later." He congratulated himself with a gulp of beer on that one.

"For your services, too?"

She was definitely keeping him on his toes. "If you'll bill me for design time for the Angel's logo, and personal-shopper time for my clothes and take the salary I should be paying you for working the truck… Actually, you should be getting a percentage of the proceeds, so, yeah, we can work that up."

Tabitha's chuckle stopped him.

"You win, Johnny. Alistair's full bill goes to you."

The urge to kiss her right then and there struck again. Kiss her hard. And long enough to last them back to the hotel, where he could get her naked and...

"So, who makes the call?"

He blinked. Saw their waitress approaching with her salad and his scrod. Fitting. Apt. He *felt* like a scrod.

"You, as my attorney, or me?" she asked. Then, as their dinner arrived, she sat back to allow room for the bowl to be placed in front of her.

Johnny salted and peppered his dish. "Do you want to call?" he asked when his mind was once again fully focused on her quest. And off her person.

"I can."

The reply, though completely typical for them, frustrated him. "I'm asking what you want."

"Oh. Then I want to," she said. "I'm not helpless."

The statement was so out of the blue, he stopped mid-bite to say, "I never thought you were."

"I know." She hadn't started to eat yet. "I just need to make sure I remember that, too."

Strong, confident, capable Tabitha was insecure. More, she'd exposed a bit of her private self to him. He was glad. And he wasn't.

With his completely unexpected attraction to her, coupled with these odd moments of charged conversation between them, things were getting more complicated by the second.

His brain told him to walk away. He had every right to—and no business continuing down a road that would only lead to a dead end when his sabbatical was over.

He could do it now. Or later, back at the hotel, which would be the decent thing to do. Let her down someplace that wasn't in public. Offer to provide an attorney in his stead. Carter Simmons would be good. And owed him a favor.

Yeah, Tabitha would get her son back and he could be on his way.

That thought passed all his mental checks. And with not one brain cell did Johnny believe he was really going to walk.

He was where he was and he was staying.

He'd just lost all appetite for the food on his plate.

Chapter Six

Tabitha called Mallory first thing Wednesday morning. If Jason and his father had been stationary for a year, there was no reason to believe that a few hours would make a difference, but to her, every second she was away from her son mattered.

The daycare owner wasn't as openly friendly as she'd been during their previous conversations. When Tabitha explained that Johnny was her lawyer and she had a legal issue to discuss with her, Mallory clearly didn't appreciate the contact. But, in the end, she agreed to meet with Tabitha and Johnny on Wednesday evening at a pub not far from the professional building that housed The Bouncing Ball. And she'd said she was bringing a man named Braden Harris with her. She didn't ask, she told.

More nervous than ever about tipping off Mark, Tabitha had requested that the meeting *not* be in the one place she really wanted to be—the building where her son spent the majority of his waking hours.

"I don't think she trusts us," Tabitha told Johnny just before eight that night as they waited at a high-top table in a back corner of the room, away from the big front window where they could be seen. Where Jason's father could recognize Mallory, or worse, Tabitha.

Not that Mark frequented bars. Or would bring his toddler son to one.

"The hope is that when she sees my credentials and hears your story, she'll change her mind about that."

Running a hand over her ponytail, letting it fall down her back, Tabitha concentrated on taking slow, even breaths. Johnny had offered to close the food truck early to give them time to shower and change before the eight o'clock meeting, but she'd opted for them to come as they were. They weren't out to impress, and the food truck was part of their story.

"I wonder who this guy is that she's bringing with her," she said to Johnny, one of several renditions of the same thought she'd shared with him throughout the day.

"Since they share the same last name, I'd guess Braden Harris is either a brother or a husband," he said, the same answer he'd given her each time she'd mentioned the unknown man.

She wasn't thinking so much about the man's relationship to Mallory as her reason for bringing him. "You think he's a cop?" she asked now. Throughout the day, she'd suggested lawyer, business partner, bodyguard.

"It wouldn't be horrible if he was a cop. It could work in our favor."

Our. Warmth spread through her. Other than Jackson, she'd never felt as close to anyone in her adult life as she did to Johnny. He was on loan from his real life; she understood that.

But for the time she had him...

His cell phone rang—a somewhat unusual occurrence as the few people who had his current cell number knew not to call him unless it was important. It took Tabitha about ten seconds to figure out that the caller was Alistair Montgomery.

Johnny mouthed the man's name to her almost immediately, but she would've known the identity from the way he assured the caller that no time was inappropriate to call. That he welcomed news any hour of the day or night.

He really and truly had her back. Just like she had his.

"Alistair is passing off his other cases to a peer so that he can be on this full-time," Johnny said, phone in hand as his call ended. Tabitha nodded, still nervous as she glanced toward the door. Mallory was due in less than five minutes.

"You don't think she's going to be a no-show, do you?"

"I suspect she'd have called if that was the case."

It wasn't the end of the world, either way. Tabitha had tipped her hand to the daycare owner in that Mallory now knew she didn't just have a daughter to enroll, but she hadn't said a word about Mark or Jackson, so they were safe there. "Don't you want to hear Alistair's news?" Johnny asked, drawing her attention back to their table.

"I assumed it's that he's working the case himself."

"He's got Mark in his sights, Tabitha. Or rather Matt, Jason's father." His gaze didn't leave her face. "As soon as he can get a clear head shot, he's going to be sending over some photos to see if you recognize him."

Heart pounding, she stared right back at him. "Matt, Mark. Jason, Jackson. That's too much to be a coincidence."

His shrug wasn't a nod, but he didn't disagree with her, either. "And Jackson?" she asked. "He's seen him? He knows he's okay?"

"He has and he does, as far as he can tell from a distance."

Johnny leaned toward her and looked for a second as if he was going to touch her. But then he picked up the glass of soda he'd ordered when they first came in. She wrapped her fingers around her tea glass, wishing he had touched her. Wishing he was holding the hand currently soaking up condensation.

"Matt's a personal trainer," he said. "He has a small gym in the same building that houses The Bouncing Ball."

"A personal trainer." Keeping her gaze locked on his, she tried to envision Mark in that line of business. He'd been in decent shape, not overweight, but she'd never known him to exercise. Or watch his diet. "His medical training would give him a basic mastery of anatomy, muscles and metabolism and how they work together," she said, refusing to get discouraged. It wasn't as though the man was stupid enough to try to find work in his own field.

"He would've needed some capital to rent the gym space and buy his equipment."

He'd walked away from the house his mother had owned and everything in it. "His mother had just died. It's possible she left him some money that didn't make it to his bank account." They knew from Detective Bentley that he'd withdrawn everything from his own account, but there hadn't been enough to open a new business.

Johnny nodded, but said nothing. She'd have felt better if he'd expressed his agreement verbally.

"Alistair saw him pick up Jason," Johnny said, and it irritated her that he didn't use Jackson's real name. Or it scared her. One of the two.

"And?"

"He said the little boy ran up to him with a grin,

handed him a piece of paper, presumably something he'd made that day, and held out his arms to be picked up."

Tears sprang to her eyes and spilled over. She couldn't help it. Couldn't find the emotional boundary that allowed her to function at work, to tend to the members of a family who'd just lost a baby. Or to help with a procedure that caused terrible pain to a small child. She cried each and every time. But she could always hold it until she was alone.

Focus on others. She reminded herself of the coping skills she'd learned in nursing school. Taking the focus off oneself also took the focus off one's own feelings.

Johnny's hand covered hers. Wanting to turn hers over, to interlock her fingers with his, she just sat there, afraid to move. Afraid he'd take his touch away.

Before she could have another thought, Mallory Harris was there, pulling out the stool on the other side and looking at Tabitha and Johnny's hands. Slipping her fingers from beneath his, Tabitha swiped quickly under her lashes and ignored how bereft she felt.

Braden Harris was Mallory's ex-husband—and the owner of the building that housed Mallory's daycare. Johnny hadn't seen that one coming. The two of them had somehow made the situation work even after their marriage disintegrated.

Not his business. Or concern. Didn't stop him from being mildly curious, but they had more important things to deal with at the moment.

"Since you didn't say how your business involves my daycare, I felt Braden should be here. If it's a structural problem, or I'm going to be hit with a lawsuit—"

"No!" Tabitha blurted before Johnny could give his prepared speech. "I'm so sorry... I would've said more on the phone, but when you hear the purpose of our visit, I think you'll understand. I hope so, anyway."

As if in tandem, Mallory and her ex-husband turned to Johnny. Good thing he was used to being Johnny on the spot.

Pulling out a couple of his official, non-food-truck business cards, he handed them over to the couple. Both Harrises took the time to read them over.

"Lead corporate attorney?" Braden was frowning now. "So your interest is in my building? Surely you don't want to take over my wife's… Mallory's space, I mean. Because we can end this real quick. She has a twenty-five-year lease and neither of us is interested in breaking that agreement."

He might have looked to Mallory to confirm that, but didn't. She was nodding anyway, giving Johnny the impression that these two were closer divorced than he'd ever been in any relationship. He glanced at Tabitha and had a flash of being that close to her.

But the idea wasn't feasible.

"Wait," Braden said. "Mal told me the two of you ran a food truck business." He looked pointedly at the uniform shirts they both wore. "And now you say you're not only a lawyer, but lead corporate attorney for Alex Brubaker? One of California's most lucrative private investors?"

So Braden had recognized his father's name. Some people did. Some didn't.

"I'm technically on sabbatical for a year." The more truth they told, the better their chances of being believed. "I'm running the food truck this year as a…favor…to someone. Tabitha helps me on her days off."

It was really quite simple when you laid it out there. Minus his sudden need to jump the bones of the woman sitting next to him. It was harder and harder to resist touching her. And not just sexually.

Something he'd think about later.

"I'm here tonight as an observer," he said, getting himself and the meeting on track. "To make sure that anything that happens between now and…later will be within the boundaries of the law to protect all parties."

"You're here to protect *us*?" Braden spoke again. The man, tall, dark haired and still in a suit, was someone Johnny might meet on a normal business day. He seemed likeable enough if you took away the edge of mistrust. Not that Johnny blamed him.

He understood his need to protect Mallory. Kind of like him and Tabitha.

Except…no. Not at all. The only similarity—and this was a key point to remember—was that neither women "belonged" to either of the two men sitting at that table.

"Protect us from what?" Mallory asked.

"If you'll let me explain…" Tabitha looked back and forth between them. "If you can just hear me out before you make any judgments…"

Johnny leaned down to pick up the binder he'd slid under his chair when they came in. Tabitha watched as he set it, unopened, in front of him. He'd been up late the night before, preparing a portfolio with the help of his tablet and the hotel's printer. She'd looked through it that morning, but hadn't said much.

To his relief. The work itself had been no big deal; it had been more for his sake than anything. Because he approached life by understanding its various components and connecting what needed to be connected. Tabitha waited, as though she expected him to present his research. He lifted a hand to her, indicating that she should start. He was there if she needed him.

Because he wanted to be.

As she began to speak, he wanted to take her hand again.

Mallory didn't leave the pub. Tabitha had given her the facts about Jackson's disappearance, and the woman was still sitting with her ex-husband at the table. Thinking that was a good thing, Tabitha glanced over at Johnny, looking for any sign as to how he thought the meeting was going.

"Here's the AMBER Alert for Jackson," Johnny said, opening the binder in front of him. He turned it and slid it across to the couple, who'd yet to do much but ask a question or two. They both studied the report, however. Tabitha hadn't gotten to the part where Mallory's Jason was her Jackson. She'd been leading up to it, but had stopped just before the big revelation. She couldn't lose this woman's support.

Jackson's life could depend on it.

"This is the Mission Viejo police report, which corroborates what Tabitha's told you." As before, both of the Harrises focused on the information Johnny had collated the night before. Thank God she didn't have to handle this without him.

She hadn't felt they didn't believe her, wasn't sure they'd need the proof, but knew that Johnny's decision to bring hard evidence had been the right one.

The timing of his presentation was a gift to her, as well, giving her a chance to calm herself and prepare for the only moment that really mattered that night.

How did she tell them what she suspected? What she knew? How did she convince them that she was right? She had to get more information. And it wasn't as if she could become a client of Mark's new business venture.

Or apply for a job cleaning his home. Or be anywhere he'd have a chance of seeing her.

The thought of how close she'd come, being at the daycare when his business was in the same building... The thought made her shudder.

"And here," Johnny said, "is an age-progressed photo of Jackson."

Tabitha started. Johnny was pushing them forward to the reveal.

"Wait." Mallory pulled the photo closer. Studied it.

"What?" Braden Harris leaned over his ex-wife's shoulder. "Have you seen him before?"

Tabitha's throat dried up as, at the same time, both of the Harrises stared at her.

"You think Jackson's in my daycare," Mallory said. She sounded horrified, but not as if she thought Tabitha was nuts.

Holding her breath, Tabitha nodded. And felt Johnny's knee press against hers under the table. It wasn't a hand-hold, but it worked. She took a breath. And then another.

"You acted like you recognized him," Braden said, glancing from his ex-wife to the photo, to Tabitha and back. "Does he remind you of one of your kids?"

Mallory looked at Tabitha, and Tabitha felt as though actual words passed between them. Mallory didn't have children of her own—that was in her bio—but she radiated a sense of nurturing. An understanding of motherhood.

Either that, or the months of incredible stress were taking their toll on Tabitha.

"Any time I gave him peas," Tabitha said, "he'd purse his lips and spit air, like this." Pursing her own lips, she made the little spitting noises. She couldn't look at Johnny, but was completely aware of the weight of his knee against hers. "Maybe you know a child who does that?"

"It's a common oral response in toddlers."

Tabitha conceded the point.

"My son has blue eyes." And blond hair, just like the boy in the copied picture she had in her purse.

"That's why you asked me about the Easter egg photo," Mallory said next, not acknowledging that Jason's eyes were blue.

Before Tabitha could say anything else, she was stopped by Braden's words. "You know who it is, Mal? You seriously think you have an abducted child in your daycare?"

The moment had come. Mallory was either going to open the door or slam it in their faces. Johnny's hand settled on Tabitha's knee under the table.

"I seriously have no idea." Mallory's words caused a whoosh of...disappointment.

No! She couldn't fail, Tabitha told herself. *Wouldn't* fail. Jackson's entire future rested on this.

"But you see the likeness, don't you?" Tabitha asked, her heart crying out for her son.

Meeting her eyes, Mallory grimaced. "Maybe." She tilted her head to the side. "But...I'm not sure."

"You think there's really a chance, Mal?" Braden asked, and the look he gave his ex-wife, the genuine respect and *knowing* that seemed to be there, made Tabitha envy them. Which was completely ridiculous, considering they were divorced.

"I think there's a chance."

Tabitha heard the words. She felt Johnny's hand squeeze her knee. And she got teary all over again.

Chapter Seven

"You know which child she's talking about." Braden's gaze was focused intently on his ex-wife.

She nodded.

"Because of the resemblance?" He nodded toward the age-progressed photo still on the table. Three glasses of tea and one soda, all on pub napkins, sat untouched.

Mallory took a moment to respond but eventually nodded again.

Johnny watched the interplay between them, forcing his mind to review the situation in spite of an odd desire to put an arm around Tabitha and take on her emotional burden. Mallory's reaction came close to convincing him that Jason was Jackson. And yet... Braden and Mallory exchanged a long glance, and then Braden asked, "Do I know him?"

Clearly the man's buy-in meant something to the day-care owner. Equally evident to Johnny was that the child's identity had some connection to Braden.

Because Mark was a tenant in his building, Johnny surmised. He wished, for Tabitha's sake, they could get on with formulating a plan that would end with her son back in her arms.

Or…Jason happy with his rightful father.

Pictures of white male two-year-olds with blond hair could resemble each other. Particularly when one was an age progression, not an actual photo. "It's Jason, Bray." Mallory's words seemed to stick in her throat.

"What?" Braden's strong blue gaze studied first Tabitha, then the photo in the page protector sitting next to the binder on the table, and then Johnny, before returning to Mallory. "Matt's Jason? You think Matt Jamison kidnapped his own son? No." He shook his head, then looked to Johnny, as though, man to man, he'd understand.

They had a last name now. Jamison.

"I know the guy," Braden continued, fully focused on Johnny. "I train with him twice a week. I'm telling you that you've got the wrong man. There's no way he'd kidnap a dog or cat, let alone a child. He's as upright as they come."

"That's not atypical behavior for someone with something to hide. You work harder to convince the people around you, and sometimes yourself, that you're a good guy." As an attorney who oversaw a slew of other attorneys in the various companies his father bought and sold, Johnny had to be able to read and deal with all kinds of people. He'd studied human behavior. He'd also done a lot of profile reading in the months he'd been traveling with Tabitha. "In this case, in a lot of ways he *is* a good guy, and the truth is always more compelling than even the best-told lies."

He'd done profiling in the unlikely event that they ever came face-to-face with the man, although he'd never actually expected to. On the outside chance Tabitha happened upon her son, the idea had been to call the police.

Johnny pulled out an enlarged version of the photo of Mark from the AMBER Alert the year before.

"Is this him?"

Braden studied the picture more closely. Longer than he should've needed to if he was certain the man in the photo wasn't his friend.

"No," he said eventually, but Johnny wasn't convinced.

"You're sure?" he asked. "If it's Mark, he's most likely changed his appearance, grown a beard or his hair, changed the color, could be wearing contacts or gotten a tattoo…"

"No," Braden insisted again, just as Mallory said, "Bray?"

She was looking at the picture.

"They're the same build," Braden said. "But the face… it's puffier."

"He could've lost some weight," Johnny pointed out.

"It *could* be him," Mallory said.

"And just as easily not," Braden responded. Then he turned to Tabitha. "I've seen Matt with Jason. They're great together."

When he saw her lips tremble, Johnny butted in. "No one's said that Mark's abusing Jackson or that he'd physically hurt him…" He added that more for Tabitha's benefit. To his way of thinking, and from what he'd read, someone who was desperate enough to commit a crime like kidnapping and then start a new life with fake identities—unless there was some tremendous provocation like saving the child from horrific trauma—was not a stable person. And unstable people acted unpredictably when provoked or when the security of the world they'd created was threatened.

"Mark was wonderful with children. He worked as a nuclear medicine technician at the children's hospital in

Mission Viejo," Tabitha said, her voice sounding strong and sure. And Johnny's overboard he-man protective instinct tucked in its tail and retreated.

Where it had come from, and why, was a distinct question, but one he'd ponder another time.

Maybe.

Probably best just to let the unwarranted he-man emotions fade into the ether from which they'd come. And never call on them again.

"I trusted Mark enough to take my son to visit his dying mother." Tabitha looked at both the Harrises now as she spoke. Emotions pushed at her again, but she was in control. Her feelings didn't matter in the greater scheme of things.

She had a life to save. And knew exactly how to school herself to get the hard work done. It was what she did many, many days when she went to work. Someone had to do the difficult jobs that ultimately kept sick children alive, that nurtured them back to health, and then that same someone had to be able to say goodbye to those children with no expectation of seeing them again.

Of all children, Jackson wasn't one she'd ever have thought she might never see again, but the duty was the same. You faced the difficult jobs necessary to save a life. And you kept your emotions under lock and key.

"You said the other day that Matt's wife died of liver disease a year ago," she began, her list in mind as she built her case. A case she'd spent much of the night running over and over in her mind. "Mark's mother died of liver disease a year ago."

Braden threw up a hand. "But…" Mallory grabbed his arm, pulling it back down, stopping his words.

With a calm she definitely didn't feel, and missing

the touch of Johnny's hand on her knee, Tabitha systematically listed the other similarities she'd found between Matt and Mark, Jason and Jackson. Then she talked about her months of searching. Of Johnny's part in her quest to find her son. She told the divorced couple how her whole world had turned on its axis the night she'd seen that egg-hunt photo on Pinterest. How that picture had affected her differently right from the beginning. How she'd looked at that little boy and known she'd looked into those eyes before. Hundreds of times, as she'd bent over that small body on the changing table, in his crib, in his stroller and cared for her son.

Then she moved on. "Mark is a nice guy, a great conversationalist. He's fun to be with," she said, watching Braden carefully, knowing now that Mallory wasn't the only one she'd have to convince to help her. Or, at least, not to inadvertently help the man posing as Matt get away with Jackson. "He's also a bit of a loner in his personal life. I didn't discover, until he'd chosen me to *become* his personal life, that he's hugely codependent. He picks one person whose constant presence in his life makes him feel safe, and that allows him to be sociable, friendly, helpful to everyone around him. I later found out that he picked me when he first learned his mother was sick."

The Harrises were listening to her. It was all she could ask for at this point. Encouraged, the intense need to reconnect with Jackson pushing at her, she continued. "When he and I first went out, it was with a group of people. We were celebrating the completion of a doctor's residency and ended up sitting together. I think now it was by his design. Then, at the staff Christmas party a few weeks later, it was the same thing. Mark knew I was alone for the holiday and invited me to celebrate with him and his family—which turned out to be only his mother, but I didn't know that at the time—and I declined. I'd spent the last several holidays volunteering at a children's home and was doing it that year, too. But he stopped by that night with some home-baked cookies and a little present for me. It wasn't much—just a package of my favorite candy bars, but the fact that he'd remembered the kind I liked and that he'd made the effort… It was so sweet."

She felt Johnny stir beside her and thought about the fact that she was telling the Harrises more than she'd ever told him about her relationship with Jackson's father. But she couldn't get sidetracked. "We started going out after that, to various hospital functions and when groups of us would get together. Our…dates were always at his instigation. It was fun and easy," she said, suddenly needing Johnny to hear this, too. To understand how she'd gotten involved with a kidnapper to begin with.

He'd never asked, and their partnership hadn't required confessions.

"No expectations. Just friends who didn't have partners and enjoyed being together." She considered the next part of the story…had a vision of a four-year-old girl who'd spent her entire life in the hospital, a patient Tabitha had cared for since the little girl's birth…she glanced down. She was prevented by law from revealing much of what had taken place. She took a breath, and then continued with what she could say. "Mark and I were involved with a case, involving the same long-term care patient. And we were both present when the patient died."

So many of the staff had been there that day that they'd filled the room and spilled out into the hallway. Doctors, too. Sweet little Carrie had touched so many lives, changed so many lives, with her ever-present grin and resilient nature.

"That night, a lot of the people we hung out with went home to their loved ones, their families. Mark knew I'd…" She shook her head. Couldn't say out loud that Carrie had been like a daughter to her—in spite of all the rules and regulations that prevented health professionals from crossing emotional boundaries. "He took me out to dinner. Because we'd both worked on the case, we could talk about it, which was what I really needed. He ordered a bottle of wine and one thing led to another…"

They'd had sex that night on the couch in her apartment. It had been a physical expression of intense emotion—a way to expel that emotion, to lose herself in feeling something other than despair—more than it was any kind of sexual attraction. And they'd used a condom.

Johnny pulled at the wet edges of the napkin under his glass of soda. Tabitha wondered how she'd ever believed those fingers should be entwined with hers. She and Johnny…they were friends. Wonderful friends.

It was when friends became more that the trouble started. She couldn't afford to lose Johnny.

She looked around the table. No one drank. And no one said a word.

"That was the only night we ever slept together." She hadn't meant to say those words. She'd thought them. But they weren't pertinent to the current situation.

She'd wanted Johnny to know, though. Even though it didn't matter at all to their relationship.

Braden took a breath, then straightened, and Tabitha waited for whatever he had to say. Again, a touch of Mallory's hand silenced him.

"That night changed Mark. It's significant that earlier the same week he'd been told that his mother's liver disease had progressed. Also of significance is that he still lived with her. He'd never gotten a place of his own, even in college. And until her liver failed, she'd always been healthy and active. There was no reason a thirty-year-old man needed to be living with her, other than the fact that she didn't want him to go, didn't want to be alone…and he didn't want to leave her."

"That doesn't sound like Matt at all," Braden interjected.

"It didn't sound like the man I thought Mark was, either, not that there's anything wrong with a man living at home, necessarily. It's just that the codependency between them was in jeopardy with Martha, Mark's mom, getting sick. And since it happened at the exact time he and I had an…intimate encounter, he was suddenly gluing himself to my side. Acting like we were a married couple intending to spend the rest of our lives together. Talking about moving in together. He was scaring me, but I got him to understand that I needed to take things slowly.

"I was trying to figure out what was going on and how to extricate myself from the situation without making things awkward at work or in our crowd. And then I didn't have to worry about any of that because he quit to take care of his mother. I had to threaten him with a restraining order to get him to stop calling me, but it worked. I didn't hear from him again until we ran into each other at the hospital one day about six months later."

"You were showing," Mallory said.

Tabitha nodded. "Mark did the math. He knew I hadn't been seeing anyone else, that I hadn't had sex in over a year before him. We'd used a condom, but…"

Johnny grabbed his soda. Downed the entire thing, then looked around, as though wanting help from the staff.

"Was he at the hospital to see you?"

Tabitha felt it should've seemed odd that Mallory had homed in on the same suspicion she'd had in the million times she'd rethought that meeting, but it didn't. The other woman seemed to be in tune with Tabitha's life—though, more likely, her nurturing personality just made her more empathetic than most.

"He was there to attend a going-away party for one of his colleagues who'd joined the Peace Corps." That was the story he'd given her. She'd known the woman slightly, knew her by name and knew she'd joined the Peace Corps. It wasn't until later, after Jackson's disappearance, that she'd wondered if there'd really been a going-away party, and then confirmed that there hadn't been. At that point, the best she could figure was that someone had tipped him off to the fact that she was pregnant. There'd been no reason for any of their peers not to mention her pregnancy to him. From what she'd understood, though, none of them had seen or heard from Mark since he'd left the hospital.

One of the officers on the case had suggested that Mark had been following her.

She hated to think that.

"Mark pressured me for parenting privileges." She forced out the words. "He wanted to attend doctor's appointments, to help financially, but I knew that until the baby was born, I could legally put him off. After that... I wasn't going to have much choice. He could compel a DNA test and I'd lose any chance of coming to an amicable agreement with him. I had absolutely no reason to believe he'd hurt Jackson, no proof whatsoever that my son would ever be in any danger with him. On the contrary, there were dozens of people who could testify that Mark was wonderful with children. I certainly couldn't use the fact that he lived with his ailing mother as a reason for him not to see his son."

She'd been trapped. Instinctively she'd known that something wasn't right with Mark, but she'd had no evidence to back that up. Earlier, when she'd threatened him with a restraining order, he'd immediately stopped harassing her. "So I told him that while I wasn't naming him on the birth certificate and wanted no money from him, if he'd leave the DNA issue alone, I'd let him have regular visitations with Jackson and would include him in major life events like birthdays, future school functions and sporting activities."

"Sounds reasonable," Mallory said.

Tabitha looked at Johnny when he grunted. "I would've advised you to get it in writing," he said, then added, "But you came up with what was probably the best-case scenario, under the circumstances." She couldn't tell what he was thinking.

She wasn't privy to his inner thoughts. Didn't expect them. And suddenly needed them.

"It worked for that first year. Mark had Jackson regularly, but never overnight because of his mother's needs. I always dropped him off and I'd usually pick him up, too, since Mark had his mother to contend with. Jackson was always fine. Never fussy or seemingly upset. He was always dry and the bottles I sent with him were empty and cleaned. That last time I dropped him off, though... Mark's mom had died, but he hadn't told me. Or anyone we knew. He seemed perfectly normal when I dropped Jackson off. I had no idea..."

Which was part of what ate at her. Shouldn't she have known? How could she *not* have known?

"The police said later that it was obvious he'd been planning to take Jackson for some time. He'd just been waiting until his mother's death. He'd made arrangements to have her buried with no visitation or services, and he'd bought the casket and grave site months before."

There'd been more. Emptied bank accounts. Visits to the dark web, visiting sites where one could learn about fake IDs. Purchase them, even. He was a smart man with a plan.

"I had refused to be his new codependent," she said now, relaying what an analyst with the police had told her. "Unfortunately, I gave birth to the perfect alternative. Like mother, like son. Jackson was the perfect gift…"

One she hadn't meant to give Mark. One she'd never forgive herself for letting go.

One she'd been looking for ever since.

Now it was time to get him back.

Chapter Eight

"So, what are you asking me to do?" Mallory Harris's tone gave nothing away. Johnny was impressed. He couldn't tell whether Tabitha had won her over or not.

She'd won consideration, at least. For Tabitha's sake, that pleased him.

"We need evidence that will lead to a warrant," he began.

"You want me to get Jason's DNA?" Mallory was frowning. "I don't think—"

"No way," Braden interjected, shaking his head. "That would—"

"No," Johnny interrupted, looking at both of them. Tabitha had done her part and it was his turn. Feeling as though her quest lay on his shoulders now, he said, "Any DNA you collect could be disallowed in court," he said. "Collecting it without Matt's knowledge could also put you in legal jeopardy." And he truly cared about that. "When we get DNA, it needs to come with the proper chain of evidence. And Tabitha and I want it to be very clear to both of you that we have no intention of involving you in anything that would create a threat to either one of you or your businesses."

He turned to Tabitha who was nodding profusely.

His task was to protect—all of them. He could do that.

"So what do you need from me?" Mallory asked again.

Tabitha's sudden clutching of his knee under the table derailed his thoughts. But only for a second. "We need information," he said. "You've already told us his last name, Jamison. That's a good start. Anything else you might notice, any conversation that could be pertinent." He nodded at Braden. As one of the trainer's clients, he could be a great help, too.

"It's not like Jason's going to be able to tell me much," Mallory said before Braden could comment. "He was only a year old when he came to us. He's just now starting to talk in complete sentences."

Tabitha jolted beside him, sitting up straighter. She'd let go of his knee, but her leg pressed against his.

"When you first met him, what words was he saying?" she asked.

Mallory shook her head slowly. "I can't remember anything specific, although I might've made some notes in his file. I have fifteen one- and two-year-olds, most of them since soon after birth. We split them up into two classes of seven, based on a number of parameters. Because Jason was a year old when he came in, I would've jotted down a few points so I could track his developmental progress to know where to place him."

Pulling a folded sheet out of her purse, Tabitha passed it to Mallory. "I copied these out of his baby book. These are the words he was saying a year ago, along with what they meant."

Johnny wished he'd been privy to that information. He'd involved her in every aspect of the Angel's Food Truck part of their enterprise from logo design to—

Emotions that had no place in his life dropped into the current meeting. He gave them the boot.

Mallory still had her head bent, studying the handwritten, slightly worn piece of unfolded notebook paper. He'd get it into a page protector when she finished. Have it ready for next time.

If there *was* a next time.

"Sha sha," she said. "I remember Jason saying that, looking up at me like he wanted something and I couldn't figure out what it was."

For real? Johnny stared, seeing the worn sheet as possible evidence now.

"It's a pretty common sound, isn't it?" Braden's tone wasn't unkind or even unfriendly. His practicality spoke to Johnny, bringing him out of the weird funk he'd begun to sink into.

"Yeah," Mallory said. "A lot of the sounds babies make when they're learning to talk are similar. You say here that he said it every time you passed a hamburger joint he recognized. He wanted French fries."

Johnny felt Tabitha's trembling knee against his. He wanted to look her in the eye. To connect, give her strength. But her entire focus was on Mallory.

"He loved them," she said.

"I remember *sha sha* in particular because his eyes were so serious when he said it, which made me think he was used to having that word understood. I asked Matt about it that night and he told me Jason was asking for potatoes."

French fries were one form of potatoes. Babies all made similar sounds. And yet...

Sha sha used by two babies for the same vegetable prepared differently would sway some members of a jury. Or a judge.

"This is the kind of stuff we need," Johnny said. "Or anything Matt might inadvertently say that the police can take to a judge, along with all the other similarities, to request a warrant for DNA samples."

"You want me to record my conversations with Matt?" Mallory asked.

Johnny shook his head before Braden could object—which, judging by the instant frown that had appeared on his face, he'd been about to do. Johnny didn't blame him. "Absolutely do not record any conversations," he said. "California is a two-party consent state, meaning that, unlike many states, in California you need consent from all parties in a conversation before you can record it. You'd be breaking the law to do anything else so, please, do not even go there. You would not only *not* be helping us, but you'd be harming yourself." He needed to be completely clear about this. To protect Tabitha, too. There could be no appearance that she was asking anyone to break the law on her behalf.

He started to sweat. Wanted a beer. He felt things were getting out of hand. Looking at pictures, visiting daycares, going home and supporting your next-door neighbor as she grieved for her missing son was no-brainer stuff. Accusing a real live man of kidnapping and involving the guy's associates, possibly even friends, involving others whose actions were completely unpredictable and out of your control—he didn't like it.

Tabitha had hardly sipped her tea and they'd yet to have dinner. She'd made him a snack from the day's leftovers as they'd closed up the truck, reminding him that they had this meeting and that he got cranky when he missed a meal. He hadn't thought anything of it at the time. But remembering now...

When had they grown so familiar with each other?

How had they reached the point where pressing knees under the table meant something?

"The truth is, we're not sure what we're looking for." Johnny didn't like that. "His last name might be all we need if the police can use it to verify that he is who he says he is. But unless he has a criminal record, it's also possible that he paid for a new identity that would pass through police databases. Keeping your eyes and ears open for anything that might be a clue, or that could, alternatively, clear Matt... We're going with the hope that when we see it, hear it, find it, we'll know."

Mallory's eyes were clouded with concern and warm with empathy as she glanced toward Tabitha.

"Then we'll take our list of coincidences to the police and hope to God it'll be enough to justify a warrant." For Tabitha's sake, he hoped that if it got as far as contacting the police, they'd have more to go on than they did at present. "We've also got a private investigator helping us, just so you know."

Braden spoke up. "Or we could find something that clears Matt, and then there'd be no reason to go to the police." His glass of tea was half empty.

Johnny leaned forward. "It's imperative that you not let Matt know Tabitha's in the area, that he's suspected of kidnapping his son or that he's being investigated," he stated in his most intimidating lawyer tone. "I cannot stress this enough."

"There's nothing illegal about looking out for a friend," Braden said, but he seemed to be feeling his way more than asserting an intention. "And Matt's become a friend."

"If he's innocent, none of this is going to hurt him. And if he's not, then you telling him will most likely cause him to run again, which will put the life of a two-year-old boy in jeopardy."

Braden didn't seem convinced enough to suit Johnny. "Let's look at this another way," he said, becoming a lawyer completely for the first time since he'd started his sabbatical. "If Tabitha's right, and Jason really is her kidnapped son, Jackson, and you knew about the possibility and refused to help, it could look like you were harboring a criminal." He was getting into the swing of it. "Here are different ways the headlines could read. Daycare Owner Helps Return Kidnapped Toddler. Daycare Owner Helps Catch Kidnapper of Child in Her Care. Or, Daycare Owner, Housed in Building Owned by Ex-Husband, Cared for Kidnapped Child—or Harbored Kidnapped Child. Or how about his one? Ex-Husband of Daycare Owner Rents Business Space to Kidnapper..."

"I'm not going to put my business reputation above loyalty to a friend," Braden said, meeting Johnny's gaze head-on. Trouble was, although Braden was shaping up to be a pain in his ass, Johnny kind of liked the guy.

Who wouldn't see value in a man who stood by his ex-wife and put friends before business?

"What about the other tenants in your building? If your business takes a hit, so, likely, will theirs. Don't they deserve your loyalty, too? And what about Mallory's business?"

Braden didn't respond.

"Say it gets out," Johnny went on, "that someone—Tabitha—suspected her kidnapped son was in Mallory's care. Even if it turns out not to be true, what if Mallory did everything she could to help that mother find peace, while also protecting the health and safety of the child in her care? But if you say something to Matt, and he does turn out to be Mark and runs...or if Mallory didn't do anything to help..."

"Enough," Mallory said as Tabitha started to fidget beside him. "Get the testosterone brain off the table for a minute." She softened the words with a sincere-sounding, "Please."

She looked at her ex-husband. "I know you're training with Matt, and I won't ask you not to, but I think everything else in this situation is my call."

Braden met his ex-wife's eye. For a very long moment.

Johnny watched with interest, amazement, even. He'd known a lot of divorced couples, had studied difficult cases in law school, and had never seen anything like this. They seemed to have a divorce agreement much like the relationship compromises worked out between still-married couples. The most impressive part was that it appeared to work for them.

Just being there together seemed to proclaim that.

For a second, he envied them...

Braden nodded, conceding that the decision on how to proceed was Mallory's. Johnny felt Tabitha stiffen beside him. She was staring at Mallory.

As if she thought they were down to the moment she'd been both dreading and needing. She didn't seem to get that they'd passed that moment a while back. Mallory was in. All that was left was the formality of a verbal agreement.

"So we can expect your complete cooperation?" He looked from Mallory to Braden.

"Of course," Mallory said, and Johnny felt the air leave Tabitha almost as though she'd been deflated. He might have made a joke, if not for the seriousness of the moment. Or put an arm around her—if he wasn't Johnny and she wasn't Tabitha of the life-quest partnership.

"Where do we begin?" Mallory asked, clearly unaware

of the strange undercurrent between Tabitha and Johnny all of a sudden.

Or, at least, Johnny's reactions. Based on the subtle changes in Tabitha's behavior, Johnny suspected the vibes weren't just his, but he could be wrong. The changes in her could easily be explained by the growing circumstantial proof of her certainty that she'd finally found her son.

"I suggest we all order some dinner." Johnny blurted the first thing that came to mind that he deemed appropriate.

"I agree with that." Braden smiled for the first time since joining them. "But I have to tell you, just to be fair, that I don't buy this Matt being a kidnapper stuff for a second."

"Mark had a habit of biting the right corner of his lower lip." Tabitha spoke directly to Braden. "Have you ever seen Matt do that?"

Johnny watched her, impressed that she was homing in on viable facts to compel a warrant. And, again, he felt a bit…bothered that he hadn't already known that. Was he her partner or not?

"I haven't," Braden said.

Johnny ordered a pitcher of beer for the table.

He couldn't speak for the rest of them, but he needed a drink.

Chapter Nine

"I swear to you, I will check that child carefully, every day." Mallory's tone held the kind of bone-deep promise that women gave to women. They stood together on the passenger side of Johnny's small SUV outside the pub. The guys were behind the car, also involved in conversation.

They'd had dinner together with frustratingly little conversation about Tabitha's quest. She'd made small talk while her whole purpose for being there lay like the proverbial elephant on the table between them.

"I can only imagine how horribly, impossibly hard this has to be…" Mallory took her hand. Squeezed it.

Uncomfortable with the contact, and yet strengthened and warmed by it, too, Tabitha nodded. Not trusting herself to speak, she tried to smile. To find the emotional boundaries that allowed her to get through some of life's most difficult moments.

"I'll make sure I have personal time with him every day," Mallory continued. "I'll be on the lookout for any changes in behavior, for anything he might say that could give cause for concern. I'll do my best to see that he seems as happy and well-adjusted as always."

"Does he really talk in full sentences?" The question was so hard for Tabitha to ask. All the things she'd missed—not knowing about her own son's growth, his progress…and needing to know so desperately.

"He does." Mallory nodded. "And quite confidently, as well."

Tabitha felt the tears overcoming her, and Mallory must have noticed as she gave her hand another squeeze. "I don't remember his weight and height exactly, but he's pretty much average size. All our parents have to provide proof of inoculations and regular medical exams."

The medical records… Tabitha's heart jolted and then slowed. They'd be under the assumed name, of course.

"Jackson was a little small for his age at six months," she said aloud. "But he was average at the next two visits…" The last two Tabitha had had with him.

It sounded as though the guys were wrapping up. Tabitha had to know, had to ask Mallory… "So, you really think Jason is Jackson? You believe me?"

The woman's expression never faltered. "I believe there's a possibility," Mallory said softly, her tone and her gaze overflowing with compassion. "It won't hurt Jason to have me watching over him, even if he's not Jackson. And I won't be giving you any information that could put me in legal jeopardy," she added, referring back to the only real conversation they'd had about Tabitha's quest once dinner was ordered. Johnny had provided a rundown on things Mallory and Braden should and shouldn't do.

Tabitha wanted more. Needed more. Hoped for more. But it was more than she'd had that morning. A thousand times more. "Thank you."

Johnny was almost at his car door, while Braden waited for Mallory.

Johnny and Tabitha would be heading back to Mission

Viejo the next day—Tabitha was on the weekend shift again, Friday, Saturday and Sunday. Her task now was to compile a list of everything she could remember about Jackson and Mark—mannerisms, word choices, likes and dislikes. Anything that might lead them to something significant that Mark and Matt had in common, even if it was just so many similarities that they'd be hard to explain as mere coincidence.

"I'll see you Monday night, then," Tabitha said, giving Mallory's hand one last squeeze before turning toward her door. The two couples had agreed to meet for dinner again the first night Tabitha and Johnny were back in town.

"Tabitha?" Mallory called her back.

Tabitha turned.

"Jason has blue eyes," she said, her voice, even her lips, trembling. And then, before Tabitha could so much as thank her for offering renewed hope, Mallory was gone.

On the drive back to the hotel, Johnny waited for Tabitha to say something…anything. Even "They seemed like a nice couple" would've been good.

His mind spun with all the things he wanted from her—conversations he wanted to have. What had she thought about the fact that the Harrises were divorced but still appeared to be friends? Was it because, like him and Tabitha, they were close without any of the messy stuff getting in the way?

In friendship. Not in love.

Glancing at her, he got nothing. Not a glance back. And not a clue as to what she was thinking. The meeting had gone as well or better than she could have expected. She had exactly what she wanted. An "in."

If that "in" produced no more than what they'd ended up with every other time she'd been on this quest, at every other daycare they'd visited, then nothing was lost.

For now, she believed, and she'd managed to convince others to give her the benefit of the doubt.

He wanted to call her out on not telling him everything regarding her quest. Because not knowing made it harder for him to help her. He couldn't watch her back if he didn't know what was behind her.

He wanted to talk about the list she had to compile. He had some ideas, some suggestions, for an approach that would be concise, and also for ways to bring back the memories she'd need to make the most complete list.

He did neither. He drove.

And when they reached their suite, when she gave her little half wave, alerting him to the fact that she was leaving him until morning, he almost let her go.

"Hey," he called instead, standing in the middle of their shared living room. The night before they'd had wine together there. Sat together.

They'd seemed far closer than they did right now.

At her door she turned. "I'm sorry, Johnny," she said, her face creased with concern. "I didn't ask what time you want to head out in the morning. Let me know and I'll be ready…"

He didn't care about the damned time.

"You okay?"

"Of course. Just a bit overwhelmed…but it went well."

Hands in the pockets of his jeans, he stood there, feeling like an idiot. Needing to go into that room with her. Into her life.

He wanted to take a shower with her. To hold her. To kiss her until she forgot the pain of her son's disappearance—even if only to give her a few minutes of relief.

"Can you be ready by seven thirty?" he asked.

"Of course," she said again.

Her smile almost felt like an insult. Which was ludicrous. Angry with himself now, he nodded and turned away.

"Johnny?" He grew hard as she called his name. Did she need him, too? In spite of all the reasons they shouldn't be lovers? Still facing his bedroom door, he glanced back at her.

"Thank you," she said, and when her voice faltered, she quickly went inside her room, shutting the door.

Her voice wavering—that was what he'd been needing. A reminder of the real Tabitha. The one who lived inside her, so completely alone.

And that was when he knew how seriously he was in trouble.

He didn't just want to be in Tabitha's pants, he wanted to share her hell.

Tabitha's mind raced as she sat beside Johnny in his SUV on the way home Thursday morning. Since they'd made arrangements to run the food truck in San Diego for the next month and had rented the prep kitchen with approved parking, there was no reason to drive the truck back and forth. No need to tow the car.

There was so much on her mind. First and foremost, hearing back from Detective Bentley, whom she'd called first thing, to tell him about Matt Jamison. Then there was the list she had to make for Mallory and Braden Harris. Johnny had already warned her that if Mark had bought his new identity from a good source, he'd pass the background check.

The key to getting her son back was DNA, the only definitive proof, and to get that they had to have compelling evidence. She kept thinking that the break they needed could very well lie within her own mind. All it would take was for her to remember something pertinent, something that would convince a judge that Mark and Matt were probably the same man…

And, she reminded herself, she was going to be spending the next four nights alone.

Funny, when she'd left home Saturday night, going back hadn't been an issue for her. Other than the wonderful, far too short year she'd had with Jackson, she'd been living alone for years.

And traveling with Johnny for months. Spending nights on the road sharing a suite with him. So why, suddenly, was she upset because he wouldn't be in the room beside hers that night? Why did the next few nights loom so heavily before her?

Was she becoming some kind of weakling? Thinking she needed someone to take care of her?

It wasn't like he was going to be heading across town someplace unknown to her, to his real life. He'd be where he'd been since she met him, in his house right next door. Not much farther away than his room on the other side of any number of hotel suites they'd shared.

He'd been quiet all morning. Almost to the point of weirdness. Did he know how much she'd been relying on him—emotionally—over the past week? Had he sensed a change in her?

She didn't blame him for pulling back. In another three months he'd be resuming a life she knew nothing about and had no role in. He couldn't have her getting clingy. She suspected that if Johnny sensed her growing attachment to him, he'd distance himself for her sake. He wasn't a guy who'd lead her on or start something if he felt she'd be hurt in the end.

Hopefully, very soon, she was going to be consumed with raising her son—becoming reacquainted with him, helping him through any emotional issues caused by the sudden life change that would be descending upon him. Being patient while he got to know her again…

Her stomach lurched at that last thought. Then she was back to worrying about having screwed things up with Johnny.

Their relationship couldn't get messy. She understood that. Wished there was some way she could let him know they were okay without making it uncomfortable between them.

She had no idea what he and Braden had talked about as they left the restaurant the night before. No idea how Johnny thought the meeting had gone. What he thought of the Harrises. Or her chances of getting Jackson back. And because of the sudden distance between them, one she feared she'd created, she didn't ask him any of those questions. How he felt, personally, wasn't going to change anything. If he'd had legal concerns, he'd have told her. She had to stay focused.

Half an hour from home she could hardly stand the tension anymore.

"Are you okay?" The question was a watered-down version of what she really wanted to know. Were *they* okay? And it was the same question he'd asked her not long ago.

"Of course." Same answer she'd given him… He didn't take his eyes off the road long enough to glance at her.

She told herself to let it go. Things had been a lot more intense this trip. He probably just needed a break from her part of the life-quest partnership. Needed some time away from her.

But she had to ask, "Are you angry about something? Angry with me?"

It mattered to her. Whether it should or not. If she'd screwed things up, she had to try to fix them. He was worth it. Their partnership was worth it.

At least to her.

"No."

Let it go. They were twenty-five minutes from home. And then she'd be working three twelves in a row.

"You seem different," she said.

With a shrug, he shook his head. "Still me."

"Johnny…"

Finally, he glanced her way.

"Tell me what's going on. I can't lose you." No! Those weren't the words she'd meant to say. She held her breath, needing to take them back and afraid that if she tried, she'd only make everything worse.

"Of course you can. We both knew this was just for a year. I've got my life to go back to. You've got yours…"

He was only reiterating what she'd been telling herself all morning.

"I can't lose you *yet*," she qualified, fearing, even as she said the words, that they were a lie. She couldn't lose him ever.

But *ever* wasn't here. *Now* was. She had to deal with now.

Who knew how she'd feel when Jackson was back in her life? When Johnny donned his suits and ties and became corporate lawyer man again, living in a different world, *his* world. One she knew she wouldn't be happy in. Wouldn't fit in.

"You don't seem to need me all that much," he muttered.

What? She stared at him. Had he sounded a bit…petulant? Johnny? She must have misunderstood.

"Could you clarify that statement?" Now she was the one sounding all distant and businesslike, but she was truly perplexed.

"I'm just saying…this partnership, working together to reach our individual goals—the idea was that it was supposed to be fifty–fifty."

"And you think I'm not keeping up my end of the bargain?" As she thought back over the weekend, a wave of heat followed by cold washed over her. "Johnny, I know I messed up an order, dropped food in the truck and probably wasn't as fast as I usually am, but I swear to you, I'm committed to seeing the Angel's Food Bowls truck make the money you've set as your goal. Her truck will be a proven success and a huge boon to local charities. I promise you…"

He was shaking his head again and she stopped. With everything they'd done, the business they'd already built, he could continue alone, hire someone to take orders at the window, and he'd still reach his goal before his year was up. Was he ready to end their partnership now? Trying to tell her they were through?

In truth, he hadn't signed on to be volunteer legal counsel to her and a divorced couple they'd only just met. And then there was the investigator. She had to pay his bill immediately—so Johnny would know she wasn't going to take more than she gave…

"I involved you in every aspect of my project, even down to wardrobe," he said.

"I realize that, Johnny. And I'm happy to do my part. Whatever you need, just say it."

He was still shaking his head.

"What?"

"Forget it."

"No." She was going to get angry in a minute. If their partnership was at risk, they couldn't simply walk away. "Tell me what's on your mind."

He'd stopped at a red light and turned to face her. "You sure you want to know?"

More was going on than her not doing her part. It felt as if they were getting ready to cross a boundary that, once crossed, would disappear forever. It felt like he was giving her the chance to back down. Bow out. Now. Before irrevocable changes happened between them.

But the change had already happened. Looking him in the eye, she saw that.

"Yes," she told him. "I want to know."

"Okay, just remember you asked for it."

She nodded. The light turned green and he pulled ahead. She watched the road, too, every muscle in her body tightened with fear for them, bracing herself.

"I'm pissed off," he said mildly—and yet in true Johnny style. She understood. He *was* angry. He just wasn't holding her accountable for it. Because their partnership didn't have a place for them to be angry at each other. Their partnership required that they walk away from the heavy stuff.

She almost chuckled hysterically as she had that thought. They were paying homage to his dead wife, helping him grieve in the only way he knew how. They were searching for her abducted son and doing whatever it took to bring him safely home. Did it get any heavier than that?

And yet, the heaviness they both carried was the reason their partnership had to have its step-away point. The emotional boundaries they'd put on their friendship gave them the space to help each other. The boundaries were what made the partnership work.

Now was the time for her to be quiet. They were almost home. They'd have three full days apart if they wanted and needed them. She strongly considered the option.

Part of her needed that option. The week had drained her. She had to get back to work, to find her strength.

"Tell me why you're pissed off." Another part of her needed *him*. What scared her was that the needy part seemed to be the driving force within her where he was concerned.

"I've involved you fully in my project, and yet you hold out on me. Last night, sitting at that table, I felt like a fool. I'm there as your partner in all of this, thinking you need my expertise, offering it to a couple of total strangers on your behalf, and then I listen as you give them more facts about the case we're handling than you've ever given me."

Thinking back over the night before, she knew when it had gone wrong for her and Johnny. It was when she'd talked about sleeping with Mark.

"I didn't realize until last night that the details of Jackson's conception could be pertinent. You knew what mattered, Johnny."

"I'm not talking about that, although from here on in, understand that it's important I know *everything* about the man. If Mark is Matt, I have to know everything you know…"

She nodded. Then, because he was driving and couldn't see her response, she said, "Okay."

But that hadn't really been what he was talking about, was it?

"So, why were you angry?"

"You pulled a sheet of paper out of your purse, something you've been carrying around for months, based on how folded and wrinkled it was. The information on that paper could help us identify Jackson when we find him, and you never even told me you had it."

The sheet, on which she'd copied down Jackson's words and sounds from his baby book. Johnny was right. She just hadn't thought...

"And that characteristic you said Mark had, of biting his lower lip...again, an identifier that could be pertinent."

Oh. She could see the validity of his concern. "From here on out, I tell you everything," she said. But in her own defense...

"You didn't involve me in every aspect of *your* quest, Johnny."

"Of course I did," he said immediately, still sounding peeved.

"No, you didn't." Because they'd each had areas they'd handled themselves.

"Like what?"

"The permits. Licenses. Testing. The first couple of months, other than when I helped with clothes and things, you did practically everything on your own."

"I told you about the tests you had to take." He sounded almost petulant again and she kind of felt like smiling.

"Johnny..."

They'd pulled into her driveway. He turned off the engine, even though he'd be starting it again to park next door in his own garage. Usually he kept it running. Usually she opened her door as soon as he stopped in her drive.

"You're right," he said, facing her. "I'm sorry. But what we're getting into now, involving others, accusing someone who could turn out to be an innocent man of kidnapping... Like I said, I have to know everything if I'm going to hold up my end of our deal."

Oh, God. He was in as deeply as she was. She heard it in his voice. Saw it in his eyes. They really were partners. For now, anyway.

She nodded. And knew that one of them had to rescue them from the moment before things got too complicated. His being so upset with her was enough of a threat to their partnership for one day. For a lifetime. "So...did we just have our first fight?" she asked, smiling at him.

He smiled back. "I guess we did."

And they'd made it through. Her relief was potent. She felt like an idiot, sitting there grinning. She opened the door. Johnny got out, too, as he always did, to get her bag from the back. He set it down and pulled up the roller handle.

"I mean it, Tabitha. That list you're making... I think we should do it together. Not only do I need to know everything that's on it, but I can ask questions, help you clear your mind, so we get as much as possible down on paper. The more we have, the better our chances."

We. The more *we* have.

The man was so dear to her, and an enigma, too. If she wasn't careful she was going to become addicted to him.

"To tell you the truth, I'd rather do it together," she told him.

"Good. Then, my suggestion is that each night, when you get home from work, I'll have dinner ready and we can work until you need to go to bed. That way you'll feel more relaxed about remembering everything you can and actually be able to get some rest, too."

Tears sprang to her eyes. She felt so...cared for. Beyond the casual friendships, which were all she'd had for so many years.

Still...

"I'm sure you have better things to do than cook dinner for me." Although his grilled steak was the best she'd ever eaten.

He was getting back into his car, but stopped to give her a pure Johnny grin. "In the first place, I didn't say I'd be cooking dinner, only providing it, and in the second, I'm a little bored over there now that the food truck's running so smoothly. I'm spending half the time I used to on advertising. I've got the ordering and picking up supplies down to less than a day. And now that we're staying in one place, I won't have to search out venues and worry about permits for the next few weeks, either…"

"So…you want to start tonight?" she asked him. She didn't have to be at work until seven in the morning, but had laundry to do. Grocery shopping. And her house hadn't been dusted or the bathrooms cleaned in a couple of weeks.

"Why don't we have dinner at my place tonight and then yours on the nights you work?" he suggested.

He didn't seem to be in any more of a hurry to leave than she was to have him go. But they both had things to do.

Agreeing to be at his place at six, Tabitha waved at him and listened as he started his SUV and pulled out of the drive. She was inside her house by the time he'd parked next door, but she could still feel him with her. Inside her heart.

And she knew that when this was all over, when she had Jackson consuming her days and he had his life consuming his, she was still going to care about him.

She was going to miss him like crazy, but she'd have Jackson.

Life with her son was all she'd wanted for a long time now.

Chapter Ten

They had dinner that night at his place and worked on the lists as planned. He grilled steaks, threw some potatoes in the oven and made a salad. Learning to cook had been something his mother had insisted on when Johnny was in junior high. She hadn't put her foot down often in the Brubaker household, but when she did, she got her way. Every time.

She'd insisted that no son of hers was going to be incapable of caring for himself and his home if the need ever arose. He'd spent a summer earning his allowance— enough to buy a brand-new sports car when he turned sixteen the next fall. He'd regularly cleaned the ground floor of the five-thousand-square-foot home in which the family lived. The summer before that, he'd had to help the landscapers five days a week—his father had insisted on that one.

He'd also taken lavish vacations to exotic places with his parents every summer. Some of that information she'd known already. Some she was just learning.

But it pointed out their differences so acutely. He knew how much his real life intimidated her. How uncomfortable it all made her.

She wasn't like him. Growing up with her mom and grandmother, she'd shared the household duties. She'd never been pampered and had told him she never wanted to be. Her independence, and her privacy, were too important to her. They'd had that discussion early on, just a getting-to-know-you talk about their differences.

Differences that didn't matter during this time out of time, as she'd once called it.

Very little about her life had been easy.

Other than Angel's death, he'd had a perfect life. Everything money could buy and the richness of family, too. Aunts and uncles. Cousins. A blessed upbringing by parents who not only adored him but were still in love with each other as well.

Yeah, he had everything—except drive. Passion. Maybe because he hadn't had to fight for a chance. His chances had all been given to him. That had been Angel's take on it, as he'd explained to Tabitha. But then, Angel had had chances given to her as well, and she'd been overflowing with passion.

His own version of his situation was a bit more difficult to understand. Or fix. He felt he'd been born with a deficit, a defect. Whatever it was that drove people to do crazy things, to take risks, to push themselves beyond endurance in the pursuit of a goal. He had no burning need. No fire.

Not even for the food truck, except insofar as he was doing it to honor Angel. He wanted it to be a success. He knew it would be; he'd made the commitment. But that choice had been driven by his rational mind and his sense of obligation, not by something deep inside himself.

Tabitha was driven from the inside out. Her work, the way she'd taken on the food truck, of course her search for her son…all of it came from some force deep inside her.

It was that force he was missing.

And that would eventually make him less in her eyes.

As it had in Angel's. And maybe his parents', too. Their quick approval of his announcement that he was taking a year's sabbatical to run a food truck was evidence of that. They'd been thrilled that he was determined to do this—to the point of walking away from everything else in his life. That he needed to do it badly enough to sacrifice for it. He hadn't had the heart to tell them that it wasn't about passion. Or a burning need. That it was simply his own brand of justice, the way he dealt with the fact that Angel, who'd been so filled with fire, had had her life snuffed out before she could fully live. He'd felt he owed it to her family, her parents were still some of his parents' closest friends.

In spite of his lack of passion for her, she'd still put Johnny, their families, first. *Family first* had always been his priority, too. Still was.

He and Tabitha had just finished dinner when his phone buzzed a text message. Seeing the number, he opened it immediately and watched a couple of pictures download.

Tabitha had been clearing the table and came up behind him as he looked at the first one. A man in running pants, a tight T-shirt and tennis shoes was looking toward someone off to his right.

"Who is that?"

His gut sank as he held the phone closer to her. "The text is from Alistair Montgomery," he said.

"That's Matt?" She sounded shocked. Took the phone. Stared.

"His hair's a different color and much longer. He's not wearing glasses. He's twice as buff as he was, and he's lost the little belly fat he had. His lips seem a bit more prominent, but the nose and chin… It could definitely be Mark."

It sounded to him as though she was talking herself into seeing Mark in the photo. He'd wanted her to instantly recognize the man she'd slept with. To be so certain it was Mark that he was reassured that they were on the right track. He wasn't. "Tabitha…" At what point did encouraging what might be a wild goose chase become wrong? Their partnership agreement required his support. But when did support mean speaking hard truths?

With her fingers on the phone's screen she zoomed in on the photo.

"Wait," she said. Standing over her shoulder now, Johnny saw what she was focusing on. A tattoo on the man's left arm. He'd barely noticed it.

"Did Mark have a tattoo?" he asked. She'd never mentioned it. But then, there'd been other things she'd failed to tell him. Hence, their list-building plan for that night.

"No," she said, and he frowned. "Look at this," she said, zooming in closer so only the tattoo showed on the man's arm.

"It's a lily," he said.

"Yes, but see this…" She zoomed in even farther. Pointed at what looked like dots, or flakes of dust all over the flower. "It's scabbing and dry skin is flaking off," she said. "It's the second stage of tat healing. A nurse I work with got one and this stage drove her nuts. They tell you not to scratch, since new tats are at risk of infection."

"So it's new."

"Yes." She looked up at him, and the glow in her eyes made him want to kiss her. "And the lily? It was Mark's mom's favorite flower."

Again, he wanted to kiss her. Instead, he put the phone

away, loaded the dishwasher and sat down with his partner to make lists.

While she was still at Johnny's place, she had a call
from Detective Bentley. Matt Jamison appeared to be
exactly who he said he was. His car was registered, a
prior address had come up and checked out as far as the
police computer was concerned. A birth date and social
security number were listed. He'd never been arrested.
There were no fingerprints on file.

They hadn't found a birth certificate for Jason, but
for that, they needed to narrow the search to a particular county. He had someone going through the counties
in California, one by one.

Johnny hadn't been surprised by any of it, but at
Tabitha's fallen expression he told her he'd get Alistair
to take a deeper look at the information the police had
given them. Not that they'd shared any specifics. They
couldn't. But Alistair had ways of finding out things.
Johnny called him before she went home.

Friday night dinner had been at Tabitha's place. He'd
made a bourbon-based pork au jus, with shredded cauli-
flower soufflé and snow peas, which he'd carried over
from his kitchen when he saw her pull in after work.
She'd asked for seconds. And their list had grown.
She'd also given him a house key so he could cook in
her kitchen—after he'd refused to back down on his in-
sistence that after a long day's work, she needed to be
able to come home, shower, get comfy and just relax in
her own space.

He knew he'd been right to stand up to her. She was
pushing herself too hard. And there was no one around
but him to see that.

Or do anything about it.

Alistair had found out that Matt Jamison had no formal certification as a personal trainer, at least none that was easy to find. And Alistair couldn't find any college information on him, either.

Again, that didn't necessarily mean anything. It wasn't like you could type in Joe Blow's name and find out what college he'd attended, unless he'd put something on social media.

Jamison had no social media accounts that could be traced back to him.

Johnny called Tabitha at work as soon as he heard from the investigator. She'd taken hope, as he'd feared she would. And she told him that Detective Bentley had called to say no birth certificate had shown up yet for Jason.

She'd also said she was tired and looking forward to dinner. Mentioned that she'd forgotten to take out a fresh roll of paper towels and where she stored them.

Still, it was odd, to say the least, being in her home on a Saturday afternoon without her there. He was preparing the lasagna he'd chosen after remembering how, on their travels, her first choice for dinner was always Italian, followed quickly by Mexican, and that, when Italian won, she usually ordered the dish. He was accompanying it with salad greens with homemade croutons and his own version of a Caesar dressing.

For dessert he'd bought a white cake with buttercream icing—the same kind that she'd brought over for his birthday. She'd apologized—sort of—for the fact that it was store-bought, but said it was her absolute favorite so she never made cakes.

The lasagna was in the oven, the greens washed and prepared and the cake covered and on the counter. He'd set the dining room table where they'd been working rather than the two-seater in the bay window nook at the other end of her kitchen. But he thought the little table might have been nicer. More intimate.

He thought about the wine he'd purchased and retrieved a couple of glasses from the cupboard.

He looked again at the hallway leading to her bedroom. He could walk down there. Take a peek inside. Just to know if she had a king or queen. See the things that surrounded her when she slept. If she was a bedmaker or not.

No—going inside her bedroom would be an invasion of privacy. Johnny went to check the lasagna, then set the timer on his phone and let himself out.

He'd go home, call his folks, catch up on everyone in his real life. Ask about the family business, maybe have some files sent over…maybe even take on a case or two. See if he could get through an entire hour without thinking about making love with Tabitha.

And that night, after working on the list, maybe he'd head over to his side of town, to an upscale bar he knew. Meet someone who'd still want to be in his life three months from now. Someone who'd be part of the life he'd be resuming. Start getting to know her.

Yeah, he had to do something to get sex with his beautiful blonde neighbor out of his thoughts. Something besides having it with her.

He was waiting inside for her when Tabitha came through the garage door into the kitchen shortly after seven that evening. With her hair falling out of her ponytail, her wrinkled scrubs sporting a stain and her makeup long since faded, she looked heartbreakingly beautiful. And exhausted.

"Go get your shower," he told her, taking the satchel

she'd had over her shoulder and putting it on the small built-in counter by the back door. "I'll hold dinner until you're done."

He'd already poured the wine. Handed her a glass as she walked by.

"You're spoiling me, Johnny," she said, sending him a grateful glance. If only it was her gratitude that he wanted.

"It's time someone did," he told her, taking a sip from the other glass. He'd had half a notion, when he poured the wine, about making a toast. Something about their partnership and how well it was paying off for both of them. Maybe include a nuance about partnership fluidity, about how the best partnerships worked because both members were open to change.

Sipping his wine alone while she walked off, no doubt needing a shower more than she'd ever need him, was more appropriate. And, truthfully, the way he really wanted it.

Anything else and someone was going to get hurt. He needed his real life back.

She wouldn't be happy there. Not only because it was a completely different world, different lifestyle, but because eventually, like Angel, she'd be hurt by his lack of the internal driving force that transcended normal human capabilities. Or, if nothing else, bored by his lack of it.

His own hurt, he could handle, but if he hurt Tabitha...

There'd be no excuse good enough for that.

"This is delicious." Tabitha's mouth hung open as, forkful of lasagna suspended in front of her, she praised his meal.

Like the night before, she'd come to dinner in sweats and a long-sleeved cotton shirt, black sweats and white shirt both times, her face freshly scrubbed and devoid of makeup, her hair shiny and hanging over and around her shoulders.

Both nights, just looking at her had given him a hard-on.

"Lasagna's my favorite," she said, as though he didn't already know. Johnny watched the fork. Anticipated the moment the pasta would slip inside, the exact second the fork would touch her tongue and her lips would close around it.

He was in trouble. Real trouble.

Sunday night, after three twelves and working on their lists each night, Tabitha should've been exhausted to the bone. Instead, she felt a lift in her spirits as she clocked out and left the hospital with almost a spring to her step as she made her way to the employee parking lot.

She was starving and anticipating another home-cooked Johnny meal. Although, truthfully, fast-food carryout would've been fine with her. Mostly she was looking forward to an hour or two alone with him. Talking about Jackson, answering Johnny's gazillion questions about life with her son, questions designed to bring up memories from the year they'd had together. The Mark questions she wasn't looking forward to. And yet, being able to share her past with Johnny as she remembered things—such as the fact that Mark didn't like dark chocolate, only milk—made the remembering…easier.

She wished there was something she could do for Johnny. Something in addition to the relatively simple task of being his food-truck employee. In the past couple of weeks, he'd done so much more for her than they'd ever agreed upon. Meeting with Mallory, giving legal advice, paying for Alistair, just to name a few. He'd become one of her greatest sources of strength. No matter how tired she felt when she left the hospital, walking in the door to Johnny's grin always woke her right up. Gave her the mental and emotional fortitude to get through an evening of sometimes painful memories and then be able to fall asleep when her head hit the pillow.

If she didn't know how wrong it would be, she'd think she was falling in love with him. Best-friend kind of love. The feelings that lasted long after sexual attraction faded. Love that lived on even after death.

That would be wrong, though, and she knew it. Johnny was counting on a one-year partnership that would let him walk away without regret when his sabbatical was up. He needed a friend who didn't interfere with his grieving, one who would help him honor his wife, not try to replace her in his affections. One who would be perfectly fine on her own when he left.

That was what she owed him. That was what she could do for him. Keep to her part of their agreement. Be ready, willing and able to say goodbye with a smile on her face when the year was up.

That reality deflated her good mood. But only until she reminded herself that for the next three months Johnny needed her to tell him everything she could, to share her thoughts and feelings with him in regard to finding Jackson—which was pretty much every thought and feeling she had these days. With her mind back on track, she focused on the evening ahead—refining and then printing the list they'd made and the packing she had yet to do. First thing in the morning they were going to be on the road again. Spending the next six nights in the suite in San Diego, since she wasn't due at the hospital until the following Monday.

Filled with something akin to excitement, she pulled into the garage. She thought about the fact that she'd be spending six nights with Johnny, and maybe even have Jackson back home with her before she'd be driving her car again. Chiding herself for her whimsy, she wondered what they'd be having for dinner.

She felt an instant rock in her gut as she pushed open the garage door into a dark, deserted kitchen.

"Johnny?" Was he in the living room? They'd joked about ordering a pizza some night. Perhaps he'd decided not to cook?

She didn't blame him and would have gladly picked one up.

Dropping her bag on the counter by the door, she called his name again. Made her way through the dining room to the living area, turning on lights as she went.

"Johnny?" Hand to her chest, she could feel her heart pumping hard. Too fast.

Something had happened to Johnny. She couldn't breathe for a second and then, gasping for air, or maybe exhaling a sob, she ran for the front door and didn't stop until she was on his step, knocking at his door.

"Johnny?" she called again, completely overwhelmed by panic. Telling herself to calm down. To quit being such an idiot.

There was no reason to cry.

Johnny was fine.

He'd probably just had something better to do that night than cook for her and print a list. The work was almost done. He knew pretty much everything she did about Jackson and Mark.

And he had other people in his life, even if, for the past nine months, he'd chosen to have little contact with them. His sabbatical was three-quarters done. The food truck was going to exceed all goals. Perfectly natural that he'd be thinking ahead. Making moves to resume his real life.

That thought didn't help stem the tears.

There was no answer to her knock. Stubbornly she stood there, knocking again. Ringing the bell. Calling his name.

What if he was inside and in trouble? Should she call the police, ask for a wellness check?

And if he was just out, which was more likely considering that there were no lights on except the one he usually kept burning when he was going to be out past dark, she'd show herself for the fool she was in calling the police.

Could be he'd had a call from his parents. What if one or the other of them had fallen ill? Or someone else in his family had?

Could be she'd be traveling to San Diego by herself in the morning. Staying in a much more affordable and modest hotel.

Could be...

Her phone rang. She'd failed to remove it from the front shirt pocket of her scrubs when she'd dropped her bag on the counter.

She grabbed the phone. Saw Johnny's caller ID and felt the sweetness of relief.

He was fine.

And she was fine again, too.

Chapter Eleven

Day too nice to waste. Decided to take plane up. Heading to Phoenix. Not sure when I'll be back. Don't count on dinner.

Johnny mentally replayed the text he'd sent earlier that day as he listened to the ring on the line, waiting for Tabitha to pick up. Hoping she picked up.

And hoping to God he hadn't screwed up past the point of them being able to continue on with their plans. Tabitha was such a loner, so independent… Would she shut him out once she knew he'd been so messed up he'd had to get away from their life and back into his own?

"Hello?" The sound of her voice sent spirals of relief through him. At least she was still talking to him.

"Hey, listen… I'm sorry. I had a bit of a brain fart earlier and… I've got takeout barbecue with all your favorite sides. If you haven't already picked something up…" Johnny wanted to just keep talking, to prevent her from mentioning the damning text message he'd sent, but ran out of words to string together.

He'd screwed up, gotten weird on himself, which

he still didn't understand so how could he explain it to Tabitha? He needed to reassure her it was no big deal.

But he'd sent the damned message...

"Why would I have picked something up?" She sounded perplexed. Okay, maybe his text message hadn't been as bad as he thought.

"I just—good, then... So, you haven't eaten."

"Of course not, Johnny, I don't get off until seven. It's only seven thirty. And it's not like we have some set-in-stone time limit to eat. I'll jump in the shower and be ready when you get here."

Wow. The woman was incredible. Going on as though he hadn't had a bizarre out-of-body experience that afternoon and nearly screwed everything up...

"Unless you want me to meet you at your place?" she added. There was a lilt to her voice. He liked it. A lot.

"Johnny?"

"I'll see you at your place," he told her, wiping the sweat off his brow as they ended the call. The afternoon away had done him good. Until he'd heard her voice, heard how happy she was to hear from him, and he'd realized how relieved *he* was that she wasn't holding the text he'd sent against him.

He had to talk to her. Let her know...what? That he had the hots for her so badly he'd run away from her that afternoon? That he'd purposely put himself in a position where he couldn't do what he'd told her he would?

Of course, she already knew that part, about the way he'd run off. It had been in his text message.

She hadn't asked why. She'd just been glad that he'd returned with dinner as planned. Because that was how their partnership rolled.

Too bad Johnny wasn't rolling right along with it.

* * *

Showered, in sweatpants and a big, thick gray sweatshirt—chosen because she could go braless in it and hadn't been able to bear strapping herself up again that night—Tabitha picked up her phone. She was ready to leave her small master suite and head to the dining room. She could smell barbecue and mac and cheese. Johnny had arrived...

And her phone's new-text icon showed on the screen. She'd just left work, so no need for FYI messages from the hospital. If there'd been an emergency pertaining to something she'd done that day, they would've called. So who'd be texting her? Except... *Mallory?*

Clicking to open her text app, she stood in the middle of her room, willing her hands to stop trembling. She'd given the other woman her cell number...just in case.

Johnny's caller ID icon appeared on the new text. She could breathe again.

Smiling, she took a couple of steps toward the door, opening the message. He was probably sending some unnecessary apology for having been late.

As if she had any right—or desire—to...

Day too nice to waste. Decided to take plane up. Heading to Phoenix. Not sure when I'll be back. Don't count on dinner.

Slippered feet frozen in place, one in front of the other, Tabitha continued to stand there, reading the message a second time. Johnny hadn't called because he was running late; he'd called because he thought she wasn't expecting him at all.

Heart pounding, she took a deep breath. He didn't owe her dinner. Or anything. He'd had a free Sunday and...

Had he been planning to get back in time to drive to

San Diego in the morning, as planned? They weren't opening the food truck until dinner. But there was nothing that said he had to open it at all the next day. Or ever.

They'd been planning to meet Mallory and Braden to go over her lists...

But Johnny's real life had called out to him and he'd answered the call. He owed her nothing; he could end everything at any time. There was no law that said he had to live next door to her for the entire year he'd set aside for himself.

"Tabitha?" Johnny's voice sounded in the hall, as if he was heading toward her bedroom door. Looking up, she saw him standing there, his gaze locked on the phone in her hand.

She might have gasped when she first read the text. Might have made a sound. She didn't know what had brought him to her.

"You've been out of the shower a long time," he was saying, still looking at her hand. "I was just checking to make sure you were okay." He raised his eyes to meet hers.

"You own a plane?" It was the only thing she could get out. The only thing she wanted to focus on.

He wasn't just rich. He was...completely out of her league.

The relationship between her and Johnny had been different lately. Changing. She'd worried about it. And then she hadn't. The past three days had been great...

For her.

"Technically my family owns it," he said, his hands in his jeans pockets now as he stood in the doorway facing her.

Another time she might have felt awkward having a man in the doorway of her bedroom. As much as she'd come to care for Johnny, she probably would've been a little uncomfortable having *him* there. At the moment, the bed behind her mattered not at all.

"Your family owns a plane."

Forget about the plane, already! Who cares about a plane?

"Yes." He nodded. His shirt, cream-colored and with a denim-like texture, fit his shoulders to perfection, making him look…manly. She'd been thinking about those shoulders a lot. Thinking about those arms. About him holding her. About laying her head on his shoulder and letting him take care of her for the second or two she'd need to regain her usual strength.

Had he sensed her out-of-character neediness? Been repulsed by it?

"A four-seater? Like a Cessna?" Some only moderately rich people had them. But was he a pilot? As well as a corporate attorney and an only child with a dead wife to grieve for? Didn't he know how dangerous those small planes could be?

"A twelve-passenger corporate jet."

Tabitha's knees felt like they were going to give out on her. She had no intention of letting them. "So, you hire a pilot to fly it?"

What kind of family business allowed for such expenses? He'd said his father was rich enough to have people work for him. That he made his money by investing in various projects. She'd never imagined enough magnitude to support a corporate jet. Johnny's other life was out of bounds for her. She'd understood that from the beginning. Was fine with it.

But…he and his family owned a corporate *jet*? One he could just take out on a Sunday-afternoon lark? To Phoenix?

Was he getting a kick out of driving her around the state in the little SUV he'd purchased for his sabbatical?

"We have a full-time pilot on staff," he told her, shoulders a bit hunched as he remained standing in her door. "But I took it up myself today."

"A twelve-passenger jet."

"Yes."

"By yourself."

He shrugged in lieu of yet another affirmative response to her sudden aeronautical fascination.

"What did you do in Phoenix?"

Who jotted off to Phoenix for the afternoon?

She'd been at work for twelve hours. He could have… done anything he wanted to. His time away was no business of hers. Even if he had some woman from his previous life that he'd flown to Phoenix to have lunch with. Maybe a friend to him and Angel?

The immediate stab of jealousy she felt dissipated when she remembered that Johnny wasn't dating at all this year as part of honoring Angel. And prior to that, he'd been a married man.

There'd be no other woman to make her jealous. Not yet.

"I sent that text late this morning," he said, side-stepping his time in Phoenix, sending another stab of…insecurity where her relationship with him was concerned. And envy, too. Any woman Johnny would fly to see would be one of the luckiest women on earth. Whether that happened now or in three months.

The man had a corporate jet that he could "take up" on a whim. No one she knew lived like that. Johnny Brubaker was so far out of her realm, she couldn't imagine what it must be like to live in his real life.

Or to spend a day in Phoenix with him.

"I didn't land in Phoenix," he said into the silence that had fallen.

"Where did you land, then?" They had to talk, to get out of that moment so they could get out of her bedroom. And back to—or on to—whatever came next.

Did she dare hope he'd still be going to San Diego with her the next day? And that he'd be with her for dinner with the Harrises?

Did he find her too ordinary? Maybe he felt sorry for her behind her back, living the way she did. It probably seemed to him that she was on the verge of poverty. She owed money on her house. On her little car.

He had a corporate jet.

Was she wrong to cling to him if he'd determined it was time for him to move on?

She still had three months with him.

Unless he'd decided to end his sabbatical early.

Fear struck her again.

"I'm sorry, Tabitha."

For leaving their partnership ahead of time? "You don't owe me any apologies, Johnny." She had to assure him of that much. "You've been…a godsend and…"

She was *not* going to cry. She'd found Jackson. She just had to believe that. The rest, getting her son home— that work would be small in comparison. And the result immense. Beyond important. She could…

"Where did you land?" she asked him.

If he'd resumed his old life early, if he was even thinking about it, she had to support him. So she would. As soon as he told her what she was supporting.

"I didn't land. I circled the airport in Mesa where we usually land and I turned around and came back. There's a golf course there I like. I'd thought about playing a round, but decided against it."

She didn't react for a second. He had a jet. Could fly it. Had flown to Arizona and back. But before he'd left, he'd texted to tell her he wouldn't be home.

She glanced at her phone again. Had he been coming back at all? The message said he wasn't sure when...

"I'm said I'm sorry. I... Dammit, Tabitha, I sent that text this morning. Why are you only looking at it now?"

She bristled at his tone of voice. As though it was *her* fault, somehow, that she was feeling like crap. It was, of course. She'd had no business starting to...want him as a permanent part of her life. To picture him playing with Jackson sometime. Maybe coming to one of his games in the future. To think about calling him now and then just to say hello.

As friends only. She wasn't so far gone as to think there'd be more. She'd never be happy in his world.

No one in her circle randomly called guys who owned jets just to say hello. If ever she'd needed the reminder that her life and Johnny's real life didn't coincide, that moment was it. Burning up with humiliation, she said, "The text only showed up a couple of minutes ago."

Pulling his hand from his pocket, he threw it in the air. "How could that be? I sent it *hours* ago!"

So now it was the text's fault?

"I...don't always get my texts right away in the hospital. And I put my phone on data-saver mode last night because I got a notice from the phone company that I've almost used up my plan's allotted amount for the month. It connects to my wi-fi when I'm at home. With all the stuff I did while we were in San Diego last week, the things I looked up and the research and—" When she heard herself sounding like she was whining, she stopped. Just shut right up.

He flew off on a whim, and she had to use data-saver.

He ran his hand through his hair and then slid it back into his pocket. Was the barbecue getting cold? They should probably go eat. She stared at him.

He stared back. There were clearly things he wasn't telling her. If she forced the issue, would she lose him sooner?

"Were you planning to be back in time to head out in the morning?"

"I didn't know."

Biting her lower lip, she nodded. So she was right... he was already starting to pull away. To return to his real life.

She couldn't blame him. As his friend, as someone who truly cared about him, she had to encourage him. The best part of her was glad that he was healed to the point of hearing his life calling to him.

"And now? Are you still planning to go to San Diego in the morning?"

"Absolutely." His gaze didn't waver as he added, "I'm not going to leave you in the lurch."

Something he'd decided that day? At the moment, she wasn't going to question him about it. But she would later. Sometime that week they'd have the conversation. And she'd find a way to let him go.

She nodded, took a step toward him, toward the door, to move down the hall and back out to the room they'd shared the previous two nights—her kitchen. "Is dinner ready?"

He didn't step aside. Not even when she was standing directly in front of him. "I mean it, Tabitha. I'm going to see this through with you." His look was so intense, she had to swallow. Wet her lips.

And then she smiled. "I know," she said. And she did. Ultimately, Johnny would always do what he said he was going to do. Including taking up his old life as soon as his year was out.

Which meant it would be up to her to set him free.

And she would.

As soon as she figured out how…

Chapter Twelve

Johnny had to hand it to Tabitha. Driving to San Diego, shopping for perishables, working side by side in the rented kitchen on Monday, preparing to open for dinner that evening—during all of it, she was congenial, helpful as always, efficient. She even reminded him to eat something as they cleaned up the day's leftovers to carry him over until they met Mallory and Braden for a late supper.

Everything the partnership required.

And nothing else.

There were no long glances between them. No touching, not even brushing by each other as they worked in the truck. And not a single word of non-life-quest conversation.

The lady had class.

And enough inner strength to see her through any hurricane that might hit her shores.

She'd also clearly changed toward him since reading his text the night before. The partnership was intact; he couldn't say as much for whatever friendship had developed between them. When he'd first seen her standing there, staring at her phone, when she'd looked up at him, he'd been slammed like he'd never been slammed before.

It was a look he'd never forget. One he didn't want to re-member. One he wished he'd never seen.

What the hell was going on with him? He didn't know. But he was going to do something about it. As soon as he figured out what that something was.

Or...he could leave things as they were. Finish out the partnership—nice and clean, based on the day they'd had—and then sever it as planned.

He could if he didn't constantly have to fight the urge to take her in his arms.

If he didn't feel the tension in her as they pulled up to the pub to meet Braden and Mallory. The same place they'd been the night they'd met the other couple for the first time.

If he didn't care so much that she was struggling all alone.

Alistair Montgomery had called that evening as they were parking the truck. Tabitha had heard the PI say that so far, he'd found nothing. He'd even questioned whether Johnny still wanted him on the payroll. According to him, Jason and Matt were a "melt your heart" father and son. Johnny had translated that to melt a *judge's* heart. There wasn't a hint of any cause for a warrant based on the child's safety or well-being.

He and Johnny both found it odd that, other than one previous address, and his current one, they couldn't find anything on Matt—no birth certificate and no family that came up when he searched his name, but not all coun-ties had everything available on the internet, and Matt could've been born anywhere. Alistair couldn't find a social security number, which would have allowed him to deepen his search. Maybe he'd only rented places to live and never bought a home or owned a business. The gym he was running wasn't an LLC, which could be a red flag, but not enough of one to do anything with. It wasn't illegal not to incorporate. Stupid, maybe. Foolish in terms of federal taxes. But not illegal. If they could find out where he said he was born, they could do more. Or if they knew where he'd gone to school…

Alistair had looked for the death certificate of a woman with the last name of Jamison who'd died a year ago, but had come up with nothing.

Detective Bentley still hadn't found a birth certificate for Jason.

So they had a last name but, basically, were right back where they'd been without it. If they could find information on the man they could possibly prove that he was who he said he was. But not finding it didn't mean he was living under an assumed identity. It just meant he'd done nothing in his life that involved easily searchable public records.

Tabitha hadn't said a word after Montgomery had hung up. Other than to thank him for keeping the investigator on and saying she'd make arrangements to pay his bill.

Johnny had no intention of giving her the bill. But he hadn't seen much point in saying so at the time.

"Our list is good," he told her as they exited the vehicle and walked across the parking lot toward their meeting. "Thorough. There's every chance that if Mark is Matt, they'll be able to use the list to identify him—or at least ask questions that will lead to evidence that'll help us."

Hugging her folder with the printed pages to her purple shirt, she glanced at him. Nodded.

"Jackson will have changed a lot in a year," he said, keeping pace with her. "Don't be disappointed if Mallory doesn't immediately recognize something from that list."

Her gaze in front of her, she nodded again. Whatever

she was thinking, she was keeping to herself. Which made him feel kind of pissed off.

At himself, mostly, but…

He touched her arm. She gave a start but kept walking. They were almost at the door. Mallory and Braden could be inside already, waiting for them. "Tabitha."

"Yeah?"

With a hand at her lower spine, he guided her off the entry sidewalk. "We're in this together." He wasn't sure what else to say to get them on track.

"I know."

Her response just intensified his frustration. "Well, here's something maybe you don't know," he blurted, having visions of Mallory noticing them out there and either wondering if they were having an argument or coming to the door to invite them in.

The Harrises could also walk up at any second if Johnny and Tabitha were the first to arrive…

"I care." He finished his statement more slowly. There. It was out. Not a partnership conversation at all. But out there anyway.

She was looking at him, so that, at least, was a good thing. Still not talking, though.

"Please don't shut me out."

The resolute expression that crossed her beautiful face was a surprise. For someone who read body language, who read people, fairly easily, he pretty much sucked where she was concerned. "On one condition," she told him, and he felt a flicker of relief. He'd been preparing to hear her deny shutting him out. Preparing to have her pretend that things were fine between them.

"What's that?" Conditions he could handle. Every day. He'd make a list of them if she'd like. And stick to them.

Had she noticed his growing attraction to her? Even

as the thought hit him, he dismissed it. Her current mood was because of the text message. The fact that he'd left without a clear plan to return, that he'd actually considered not joining her in San Diego for the week.

"Please be honest with me," she said.

"I've never lied to you."

"Not in words, no, but you need to communicate with me. Tell me what's going on with you, too," she clarified. "If you want out, you tell me—to my face, not in a text message, and before it's reached the point that you have to hop on a plane and fly away."

He'd never had his face slapped, but he figured he now knew what it felt like.

"That's what you think yesterday was about?" he asked. "I wasn't wanting out," he told her, trying to sound his professional best while feeling like some wet-behind-the-ears college kid.

Her expression told him she was on the verge of withdrawing from the conversation.

"Listen," he said, feeling an imminent loss closing in on him. One he had to avoid at all costs. "We can talk about my...lapse...yesterday when we're done here tonight. I'll explain, okay? For now, just lean on me, if and when you need to. Let's get through this meeting and trust that we'll work the rest of it out."

Her look was long, searching. He had no idea what she hoped to find in his face, but he tried his damnedest to make certain it was there.

"I think I deserve a second chance," he said next, feeling a return of the confidence that had been a quiet companion all his life. "I think I've earned it." He pushed a little harder.

He knew the second she capitulated. He felt it in that whoosh of released tension, the same one he'd felt while sitting beside her the night they'd first met the Harrises. Then he saw it in her smile.

And, finally, he melted with it as she put her arm through his and they walked into the pub, almost as if they were a couple.

In reality, he knew, she was just leaning on him, as he'd instructed. But for a moment, he let himself forget.

Tabitha was keyed up as she followed Johnny into their suite shortly before eleven Monday night. They'd checked in late that morning—a suite identical to the one they'd had the week before, but on a higher floor—and her things were already in her room. He'd said they were going to talk.

She planned to hold him to it.

There was no way she was going to hold him back if he was ready to resume his life. Clearly, he was an important man, a powerful man. He was wasting his time here with her.

Mallory and Braden Harris were willing to keep their eyes open for any sign that Jason could be Jackson. They'd accepted the list with promises to give it their utmost attention, but neither of them read through the pages-long collection of details while they were together. Braden did offer that he would try to find out more about their friend Matt—to rule him out, he'd said. Other than that, they couldn't do anything without the risk of endangering a child in Mallory's care by exposing him to someone who could be a crazy woman or, in any case, perceived as a crazy woman who thought she was his mother. They'd suggested Tabitha stay away from The Bouncing Ball daycare altogether.

They'd sought their own legal advice—no offense to Johnny—and had been told everything Johnny had already told them. But perhaps with a bit more doubt with regard to Tabitha. The Harrises had been kind in the delivery of their message—that they'd do what they could but were not, in any way, on Tabitha's side in this matter. They weren't taking sides at all. And they wouldn't be passing along any information that could be considered confidential or of a personal nature.

Once she got through the gist of it and had had a moment to think, Tabitha was okay with it. They weren't backing out of their agreement of the week before; they were just proceeding with caution; which Johnny had advised they do to begin with.

And it wasn't as if she'd ever asked to even see Jackson. Or *would* ask to see him until they'd gone through the proper channels. She'd lost him once due to what felt like foolishness on her part. She wouldn't let that happen again.

But now that the Harrises had their own attorney, they didn't need Johnny to protect them.

And while she cried inside at the thought of losing his friendship, she would survive and get Jackson back without him. Starting that night, if he was done with the quest of honoring his wife's dream. Maybe she was making more of the day before than she should, but as a woman who'd always stood on her own two feet, she figured she'd been given a heads up. She had to be able to go it alone. No one could fault Johnny for finishing his sabbatical early, if that was really what was going on. The dollar amount he'd chosen to arbitrarily determine success could be fluid. With the lineups they'd had again that day, he couldn't possibly see the venture as anything but a success.

They'd known all along that there was no guarantee

she'd find Jackson during the year he was helping her. Jackson back in her arms wasn't part of their agreement.

He opened a bottle of wine without asking her if she wanted any. She didn't recognize the label and wondered if it was stuff he was used to drinking at home. Higher-end than the locally made bottles they'd purchased together the week before. Higher-end than anything she'd probably ever tasted.

She thought of the number of times she'd suggested fast food to him during their travels, or an inexpensive diner, and he'd been a good sport and agreed. She'd wanted to ask if those had been the first times he'd ever had the stuff. In her mind, people with corporate jets didn't settle for cheap fare when it came to their stomachs, either.

Standing there, uncomfortable, sad and yet determined, too, Tabitha looked at the door of her room. Wishing this was just another trip on the road with Johnny. Hoping things would go back to what they'd been.

He reached for a glass, his shoulders looking strong as they stretched the purple shirt. He was a single man with an entire life she knew nothing about. How could she possibly have begun to think he was hers?

And that she was his?

They'd been on loan to each other.

She'd always known that.

A second glass appeared beside the first one, still empty, on the bar. He was intending to pour one for her, too. She suppressed a sense of giddiness.

When had Johnny ever poured for himself and not for her? He was a gentleman. Polite. Didn't mean that they were a pair. That they were together.

That they'd developed something between them on a more elemental level than a temporary partnership.

She'd been planning to stand while they talked, to accept whatever he had to tell her and then excuse herself to go to bed. It was late. They had to be awake early in the morning if they were going to be prepped, parked and ready for the lunch crowd down by the beach. But as he poured that wine her knees started to feel weak again.

She sank down on one end of the couch, sitting forward, still ready to take off to her room as soon as their business was completed.

"I bought this yesterday," Johnny said, bringing both glasses and the bottle over on a tray that he set down on the cherrywood coffee table in front of the couch. She'd mentally assigned him the seat on the other end. He took the middle. "Based on what we bought last week, I thought we'd both like it."

It was white. Not too sweet. And the smoothest wine she'd ever tasted. "It's good." She couldn't help wondering how much he'd paid for it, suspecting it was more than her grocery bill for the week and feeling guilty even as she enjoyed her second sip.

After a day in the food truck, she needed a shower. Felt far too ordinary in jeans, her food truck shirt and tennis shoes to be drinking fine wine in a plush hotel suite.

Johnny was in jeans, too. With the same kind of shirt. And hadn't showered, either. She liked him that way. And feared losing him—just as she knew she had to encourage him to go.

"You said you'd explain…about yesterday." She took another sip, holding her glass on her thigh when she was through.

He leaned forward, his glass between his hands, head lowered. But he glanced at her. Her insides jolted—with gratitude for being lucky enough to have spent the past nine months with him. To have had him as a partner in what would surely be the most important quest of her life.

She loved him.

The thought was there. Just calmly fact. She loved Johnny.

Her Johnny. Not the man who flew jets and hobnobbed with the rich and famous.

Seemed like kind of a no-brainer, really. Who *wouldn't* love him?

And, like any friend, she had to be strong enough to let him go. Maybe if she kept telling herself that, kept repeating the admonition over and over, she'd be able to do it.

She wanted to. Truly wanted what was best for him.

But she couldn't quite get a picture of her life without him.

"Johnny?"

"I've been struggling…with something for a while now."

She sipped some more wine. She held her glass, waiting, counting the beats of her heart pounding against her chest. Telling herself she wouldn't cry in front of him. That wouldn't be fair. She had another swallow of wine— welcoming the idea of a little alcohol taking the edge off, easing the pain she carried around inside her. She'd get through. She always did. What choice did she have?

Hard lessons learned from her mother's sudden death…and then Jackson's disappearance. There'd been nobody to pick up the pieces but her.

"I just…" He moved a little closer. She would've scooted over, but had nowhere to go. And then, because there was nothing she could do about it anyway, she was just plain glad of his closeness. He took her free hand. Ran his fingers along the back of it.

His touch jostled the wine in Tabitha's glass. Warmth spread through her body. He was…her Johnny.

How could she bear to lose him? Not have him to call? To watch over her? To be there when she needed him even when she didn't *know* she needed him?

"I've come down with…a distressing…"

Her heart lurched with alarm as her medical training kicked in. He was ill?

"Situation," he finished.

Relieved that he wasn't sick—and back to dreading that he was going to tell her he was ready to terminate the partnership, Tabitha took another drink of wine, embarrassing herself with a gulp rather than a sip.

Distressing situation could only mean it was going to be bad.

When Johnny suddenly dropped her hand to slide over and grab a throw pillow, then rest his arm on it on his lap, she was completely bereft. Felt as though he was already leaving her.

He was obviously struggling to tell her. She should help him. Make it easier on him. But she wasn't sure she could trust herself to speak without tears at the moment.

Really, they'd done an incredible thing forming the partnership. They'd started and were running a successful food truck business. And they'd located and put in motion the means to bring Jackson home.

How could anything else matter as much as either of those achievements?

Things could still go wrong with Jackson. There was a slight chance Jason wasn't him. Maybe she could ask Johnny to hang on just long enough for that confirmation…

Hope was born and then quickly faded as she realized how selfish that would be.

"I've been afflicted with this…apparently uncontrollable desire for your body."

She heard the words. Replayed them. Stared at Johnny the whole time, trembling. Adrenaline rushed through her body.

Was he asking…suggesting…

"Believe me, I've tried everything I know to distract myself. I think I'm doing well and then you lean out the window of the truck and there I am again, hard as a rock."

As soon as he said the words, her gaze went to the pillow he held. He'd grabbed it after having been close to her, touching her hand. Was it because…? *Oh, my.*

She felt delicious. Completely outside herself.

"Like now?" the wine made her ask.

Chapter Thirteen

Johnny tossed the pillow aside. There was a certain amount of embarrassment, sitting there with her looking at his extended fly. But his intense attraction had become a problem, and he wasn't going to let it interfere with the great work they were doing. With the partnership.

"How long has this been going on?" Tabitha still wasn't looking at him. Or, rather, was not looking him in the eye.

Emptying his glass, Johnny poured himself another. He held out the bottle to top up her drink and was a bit surprised, but not displeased, when she tilted her glass toward him.

So maybe the partnership would be able to deal with his…issue as successfully as they'd handled the rest of the obstacles in their path.

"I first noticed it about a week ago," he answered honestly, feeling better already with the problem out in the open. "It was those new jeans you had on, the ones with jewels…all that glittering. A guy can't help noticing a great ass when it's being so brightly adorned."

Wait, did that sound like he was blaming her for his

inappropriate reaction? He wasn't. He was about to tell her so when she asked, "So you think I have a nice butt?"

Oh, Lordy. She was throwing him for a loop here. "Of course you have a nice butt."

She shrugged. "Well, thank you. I guess…"

"I swear to you I have not been lusting after you for nine months."

"I didn't think you had."

He took another sip. Might've done better to have picked up a fifth of something. The wine wasn't doing enough to numb his senses. As it was, he saw an icy shower in his imminent future.

"That's why I left yesterday. I woke up with a hard-on. Thought about dinner with you, got hard again. Started to pack for the week, and there it was *again*. I needed one hell of a distraction. The jet was it."

"Did it work?"

Motioning to his fly with the glass in his hand he asked, "What do you think?"

She nodded, looking like she might smile, but she didn't.

"You intended to come back all along."

"I didn't know if it would be in time to leave in the morning, but yes." The fact that she asked the question told him she'd had doubts. Which bothered him. "Have I ever given you reason to doubt me?"

She met his gaze then. For far longer than the usual look they exchanged during partnership discussions. "No."

He felt exposed sitting there, hard as a brick, with both of them aware of his penis activity. That just made it want to be more active.

He was ready to head to the shower, but it wasn't clear whether or not they'd handled the issue sufficiently.

"So…we're good?" he asked.

She chuckled.

"What?"

"I'm not clear on this," she said. "We've established that you've developed an attraction to me, and we're just going to leave it hanging there, so to speak? Making you…physically uncomfortable on and off throughout the rest of the days we're in each other's lives?"

"I was kind of hoping it would dissipate."

"Okay. And if it doesn't?"

What the hell did she want from him?

"I've had hard-ons before, Tabitha. I know how to deal with them. It'll help not having to hide it from you anymore. Seriously, that'll ease the tension right there." He thought about sitting forward, making his situation a bit less obvious, but wasn't quite ready to lose the moment with her.

Life would be a lot fairer if Tabitha had looked as though she was even a little turned on by the conversation. He had no intention of forcing anything—of using her, in any way, to alleviate his condition. But if, by some miracle, the feelings were mutual…

"All I meant was…is there something I can do to make things more comfortable? Besides not wearing those jeans again…"

"It's not the jeans, Tabitha. They just started it. Now that the awareness is there, it's there."

"So, what do you want from me?"

The billion-dollar question. He'd promised to be honest with her. But how honest was he supposed to be?

He raised one shoulder. "You want some more wine?" He held out the bottle, hovering it over her glass, which was almost full. "Come on," he urged, adding a small amount before moving toward his own, also almost full glass. That distraction had bought him nothing. Not enough time for an answer to occur to him. Or the chance to look unconcerned. Who made a point of refilling full glasses?

"You ever think about, you know—hooking up?" Probably the worst come-on he'd ever delivered, but he wasn't seriously intending to come on to Tabitha. She was his partner. His friend. Not a woman he should start something with.

Their partnership was dissolving in three months and he sensed that Tabitha wasn't the sort of woman a guy walked away from if he was having sex with her.

But he reminded himself that he'd never felt passionate enough about anything to find it particularly difficult to walk away. Look how easily he'd left the family business, his home, his parents and family and friends, for an entire year. The same ease with which he'd left every sport he'd excelled at.

Giving his thoughts free rein while his question hung unanswered between them, Johnny reflected again on the idea of going back to his life. Finding a woman he could start seeing in the interim. Tried on the idea a second time. It didn't fit any better than it had the other night.

"We're being honest here, right?" Tabitha finally asked.

He couldn't get any harder, but his body stiffened anyway, in anticipation of what might actually happen…

"Of course. It's the only way to run a successful partnership."

She leaned forward, her elbows on her knees, holding her wineglass. Ran her tongue over her lips, as if she was nervous, and said, "In all honesty, I'm thinking about it now."

He had a strong urge to know if this was the first she'd

thought of it. Never in his life had Johnny wondered if a woman wanted him. Any woman he'd wanted had made it obvious that his feelings were returned.

Angel had made no secret of her attraction to him when they were still in high school.

Angel. He was on her quest and hitting on another woman. Or was he?

It felt more like taking care of a problem that had cropped up than anything else. Talking about his condition so that he and Tabitha could deal with it together. At least he wouldn't be secretly lusting after her anymore.

"And?"

"The last time I had unconditional sex, it was with a man who turned out to be a kidnapper. I ended up pregnant and lost my son. I'm not eager to go the unconditional route again."

The words struck him farther up than his fly. In a way that was new to him. Like he had to get up and slay dragons or something equally preposterous.

"I hope you know that if you ever need anything, whether we have sex or not, I will be there for you. Always."

"You say that now, but our agreement dissolves in three months, Johnny. A little less than that, now. Once you're back in your regular life, you might not be able to get away—or even want to. You'll have other responsibilities. Real relationships. Ones that fit your life. This time with me…it's going to fade for you. And me? I'll still be right here, living it."

She made sense, and that annoyed him. "I can guarantee you that if you ever call me, now or anytime in the future, I will answer." The conviction behind the words didn't feel familiar to him, and yet there it was.

And there *they* were. There he was, at any rate. So,

was she attracted to him or not? She'd never really said, had she?

He sat forward again—and noticed that his face was now only inches from hers.

There was one sure way to find out if she was attracted. He looked at her lips. He had to kiss them. To let them tell him what he needed to know.

"Do you think I'm crazy? I mean about this thing with the Harrises and The Bouncing Ball. With Jason being Jackson." Thoughts of sex disappeared completely at the expression on her face. Her confidence, her strength, seemed to have faded away.

"A time or two in the past week I figured *I* was crazy," he said with an attempt at a chuckle. "But you? No. Never crossed my mind."

Sitting back again, Johnny relaxed against the couch, drinking his wine more slowly as his penis settled down for the night. Tabitha needed to talk. Needed his support.

He'd promised to give it to her.

Sometimes life really was that simple.

Chapter Fourteen

She had to get to bed. Had to let him get to bed. But Johnny had poured the extra wine. He was sitting there as if he had all night. As if he *wanted* to be sitting there.

Lord help her, she wanted it, too. Just to be with him for a little while longer. "Tell me what you honestly think about all of this," she said. She needed thoughts, other than her own—but thoughts she trusted—rambling around in her mind. Or, at least, added to the mix.

Johnny might not think she was crazy, but she was driving herself nuts.

"Define *this*." His expression was calm as he laid his head back against the couch and glanced at her.

Sitting back, too, she said, "The stuff I mentioned before. The Bouncing Ball. Involving the Harrises—" and the real question "—and the chances of Jason being Jackson."

"I believe you're doing what you have to do, Tabitha. And that it would be absolutely wrong if you weren't doing it. Tragically wrong to stop now, if that's what you're considering."

"I'm not!" She couldn't. "I just can't get out of the mental loop I'm in where Jackson is concerned. I think of him, and his image springs to mind and I'm off listing all the similarities between Jackson and Jason, Mark and Matt. Those similarities are just too close, and there are too many to be coincidental. Then I play devil's advocate...and then I'm back again, listing all those similarities. It's...exhausting." She took a small sip of the wine she knew she wasn't going to finish and laid her head back, too. It felt good, being so close to him.

Felt...safe. In a completely nonboring way. She almost chuckled at herself again.

Turning her head, she looked him in the eye; she was close enough to see the ring of darker blue around the outside of his iris. Cerulean outlined by an almost midnight blue. Someone should make a painting of eyes like that. "If you were the lawyer the Harrises saw this morning, would you have warned them against helping me?"

"Absolutely not." He was completely serious as he held her gaze.

"Why not? You said before that it might just be coincidence..."

"Because as long as there's a chance that you're right, if they refuse to even observe him and his father to whatever extent they can, they *could* be held liable if anything happened to Jason in Matt's care. It's a potential lawsuit."

That sounded so Johnny. So rational. All head stuff. She depended on that from him. But... "What's your gut instinct telling you on this one?"

"I don't get a lot of strong messages in the way of feelings, you know that," he told her.

"Yeah, but you have them. Everybody does. Anyway, I'm not really talking about feelings. I want to know if you genuinely think Jason is Jackson."

She was sure of it. And yet, how did that appear from

the outside looking in? Was she too involved in her quest? Losing perspective?

But how could you ever quit looking for your child? Or following up on every possible lead? No matter how small?

"I think it's fifty-fifty," Johnny finally said, his voice a bit sad. "I see the similarities that might or might not be coincidences." He stared at the wall across from them. "I also see how difficult it would be for Mark to so quickly and successfully start a new life, one that seems solid. Especially living so close by and so soon after the abduction."

She saw that, too. "He had a lot of time to plan," she told him. "Months before Jackson was born. And then a year afterward, too. Other than taking care of his mother, he had nothing to do for the eighteen months he sat alone with her in their home, watching her waste away."

Johnny's head turned in her direction again. "I just don't want to see you get hurt."

Her smile felt a little wobbly. "I'm already hurt, Johnny."

He nodded slowly, then his gaze lowered, locking on her lips.

"I hurt so much," she said softly. "All the time."

She'd had too much to drink. She was saying things she'd never, ever expressed aloud.

"I want to help make the pain go away."

"You can help," she said, looking at his lips. Johnny wanted her. Her Johnny, not the insanely rich corporate-lawyer jet pilot.

He was so gorgeous. The kind of hot that women went for in droves. And *he* wanted *her*.

Her.

He brushed some hair off her cheek, leaving a trail of tingles with the warmth of his hand.

"Help me to not hurt, Johnny."

She knew what she was asking. Didn't care that it wasn't smart. Or good. That it had no future. This was Johnny.

His lips seemed to take forever to reach hers. She waited for him. Wanted the moment to last forever. No more pain. No more losing Johnny.

He was here. Hers. Wanting her.

His lips landed and sent a shock through her entire body. A slow-moving, sharp and yet warm shock that touched everywhere. His kiss was soft. Not invasive. Adrenaline flooded her; excitement filled her. Without warning, Johnny's arms were around her, pulling her so close she could feel his heart beat against hers. His tongue was in her mouth; one hand was in her hair, the other on her hip. He kissed as expertly as he did everything else in life and she met him, move for move. Her hands slid under his T-shirt to feel the shoulders and the chest that had drawn her attention the very first time she'd ever seen him. And every day since.

She wriggled, wanting to feel him lower down, to push her crotch against the hardness he'd shown her earlier, but he managed to keep them chest to chest, their butts still on the couch.

Tabitha groaned. Impatient. She was giving herself this moment and trying to give him what he needed, too. To ease his discomfort. Because she wanted to in the worst way.

"Johnny…" She was going to tell him. They had to just do it—before the wine wore off and she had time to think.

To remember that they'd made no plans concerning birth control. Not a risk she could afford to take.

And she'd be alone to deal with the emotional consequences of making love with him—and then losing him.

That thought slowed her down.

"I know," he said. "There's a chance this will hurt you, too."

She nodded. Damn it. She didn't want to be hurt any more. But… "A good chance," she told him, pulling back. Because while he'd be leaving her to live in a completely different world—one where he was happy, one where he fit—she'd be in the same old place, alone once again.

Unless she got Jackson back.

Then she could handle the pain of losing Johnny.

Would handle it.

For her son's sake.

Why had he ever thought he could kiss Tabitha and not pay one hell of a price for doing it?

Johnny knew the rules. For everything. Made lists of them. Created a load of them. And couldn't remember a time he'd knowingly broken a single one. Why bother? He'd never been driven to the point of needing to.

Not even for Angel's food truck. He'd played completely by the rules. And the venture was proving to be as successful as everything else he'd ever attempted.

And then there was his partnership with Tabitha. For the first time, he was facing failure. He was failing her. He couldn't understand it. Couldn't get it right. And couldn't figure that out, either.

On the surface, everything was fine between them. No more awkwardness. But no more closeness, either. They were like two boxers in their respective corners. They circled. They put on a show of shaking hands for the crowd.

In other words, they worked the truck and raked in the money.

And for the next two days, they had not one word of personal conversation.

Wednesday night, after getting back to the suite with takeout, she went into her room with her share—to shower and eat in bed with the TV on, she said. Johnny sat alone on the couch and ate every bite of his.

Food usually made him feel better.

Apparently not when it came to failure, though.

For twenty minutes he sat there staring at her closed door. Thinking about different ways to get her back out. From knocking on her door with numerous excuses to phoning her. Even calling out to her. Immediately dismissing all the options as they presented themselves, he threw away his trash and headed in to shower.

He ended up at the desk in his room, instead, tablet out and on, stylus in hand, rocking back in the chair to gaze out at the view of the harbor. When answers that were usually present remained elusive, he did the only other thing he could think of. He picked up his phone.

"Hello?" The older man picked up on the first ring. In almost a year Johnny hadn't called, outside of regularly scheduled check-ins.

"Dad?"

"Yeah, John. What's wrong, son?"

Everyone at home called him John now that he was a man. He still liked Johnny.

"Nothing," he quickly assured his father.

"You wouldn't be calling if nothing was wrong. Now don't make me worry. It's not good for my health."

Alex Brubaker's health was just fine. At sixty, he had a body equivalent to a forty-year-old's according to the doctor's report after his last physical.

"Have you ever failed at something?" Johnny asked.

Silence on the other end of the line had him re-thinking the decision to call. What the hell was he doing? Flying off in the jet. Calling his daddy. Kissing his life-quest partner. You'd think he was losing his mind.

At the moment it felt like he could be.

"So, the truck's not panning out the way you expected?" Alex said after a few long seconds, and Johnny wondered if he'd called his mother over to listen in. It wasn't like he really cared. Either his mom heard it all firsthand, or his dad would tell her later. The elder Brubakers were a team, pure and simple. He and Angel had done their best to emulate them.

"Don't take it to heart, son. This was Angel's dream, not yours. You did the right thing in giving it flight. That's what matters. It's not like you need the money. Or like she does, either."

No, what Angel had always needed was independence. Life apart from their small circle, their parents, the kids they'd grown up with. Although Johnny had been happy right where they were, she'd needed what she'd called *real life*.

Not that he'd tell their parents that.

"Actually, I was thinking about franchising the truck," he said now. "It's making far more than I projected and the lines are so long I could easily support a second truck at the same venue. But what I had in mind was selling to individuals who want to get into the business. There'd be corporate oversight, but we'd give the owners autonomy, too, within boundaries that would protect the brand. And to be true to Angel's goals, a percentage of the profits would have to go to local charities."

"You don't need my input to do any of that."

No, he didn't. The legalities of creating and expanding

a business were all in a day's work for him. His father's holdings currently numbered more than two hundred ventures, with Alex as major investor of all of them. Johnny had another twelve, in his name alone. Angel's Food Bowls, even as a national venture, would be the smallest among them.

"I've never failed at anything," Johnny said, looking out into the night. Seeing ships in the harbor. Thinking about the stories his father had told of being a young naval officer aboard a ship in San Diego.

"You work hard. You give a hundred percent to whatever you do."

"And you're blessed with intelligence and talent, Johnny," his mother's voice piped in. He couldn't help smiling at that one.

He loved his folks to death, but they were so predictable. In a totally comforting way.

"Have you ever failed at anything, Dad?"

"I've had ventures that didn't pan out as well as I liked. Think of the Critchner deal."

A fleet of container ships his father had purchased had made millions instead of the billions he'd first projected. He'd sold them off for twice as much as he'd paid for them. Johnny had handled the deal.

"I'm talking *failure*, Dad. As in not succeeding?"

"What's this all about, Johnny?" his mother asked. Anne was a worrier. "What's this talk about failure? What's going on?"

"Sometimes you reach a point when you realize the venture isn't serving you as well as you'd hoped, so you realize you don't want it anymore, and you cut your losses," his father said right after her.

Johnny wasn't concerned about *not* wanting something. Exactly the opposite.

"What about wanting it and failing to make it work?"

"I don't believe in that kind of failure."

"How can you not believe in failure? It exists." He'd always known that. Just hadn't been personally privy to the experience. "Here's an example, that while maybe over the top, explains my point. Kids get abducted and no matter how hard their parents and the cops try to find them, they aren't always successful."

Sometimes bad things happened in life and you were powerless to fix them.

"They only fail if they stop *trying* to find them."

"What if they turn up dead?" What if...in the end... Tabitha didn't find her Jackson? Or didn't find him well and happy?

"They didn't fail, then, did they? They found the child."

Alex thought they were talking analogy—something Johnny had been doing with his father since grade school. He had no idea that what Johnny had failed at was finding a child.

Failing the partnership set up to find the child.

"The results of our ventures might not be as satisfying as we'd hoped, but the only way we fail is if we quit trying," Alex added. "As long as you're trying, the chance for success is there."

His dad was right. Although the partnership with his temporary neighbor seemed to be hitting a rough patch, overall it was working. He had his food truck success. And Tabitha had a potential lead to follow on Jackson. They *weren't* failing.

He just had to keep trying.

Chapter Fifteen

They worked according to Tabitha's schedule and since she had the next weekend off she had a total of seven days before she had to be back to work.

They'd work the truck all week including the upcoming Sunday, park it and then drive home so she could go to work Monday morning, which meant she had six whole days to be close to Jackson, to share the suite with Johnny. She wanted to savor every minute of her time with Johnny.

And yet it felt as if she and Johnny were barely friends now. The partnership was thriving, but since that kiss, he hadn't looked her in the eye for more than a second. And he hadn't touched her at all. Not even brushing by her in the truck.

She understood. His physical state would become unbearable if he had to walk around with a semiconstant hard-on.

Maybe she'd been wrong to think she wouldn't be able to handle unconditional sex with him.

She'd handled everything else life had handed her. Good, bad and in between. Including tragedies that would stop a lot of people. Surely she'd get through saying good-bye to Johnny. Even if she had sex with him.

Leaving her room on Thursday morning, she made up her mind to hit on him that night. She'd get a bottle of wine—not the pricey nectar they'd had the week before, of course, but something nice that was within her budget. And she'd suggest that, instead of snacking in the truck and eating out on the way home, they close up a little early and head back to the suite for room service.

She was considering the idea of pleading fatigue so he'd be amenable to dinner in the hotel, half afraid she'd have to concoct some reason to get him to agree, when she saw him come out of his room with his phone to his ear.

Johnny on the phone wasn't all that odd. The completely serious and focused expression on his face was downright scary.

Thoughts of seduction fled immediately as she approached him.

He was telling his caller to contact him immediately with any news and then he hung up.

"Who was that?" Something told Tabitha it had to do with her. Probably the way he was looking at her…

"Montgomery."

The private investigator. Tabitha stumbled as her tennis shoe caught on the marble-tiled entryway. "What's going on?" Her skin cooled, and it felt like shards of glass were stinging her.

"Matt didn't leave at his normal time this morning. His van is still in the driveway. When the guy on night watch noticed the discrepancy, he was too late…"

"Too late?" The blood drained out of her body. She could actually feel it leaving.

"When he didn't answer the knock on the door—a

would-be wrong address for a delivery if he *had* answered—Montgomery's entire team began canvassing the area. They got a local bus driver who said Mark and the little guy boarded about six this morning. He let them off at another stop, several miles away. Montgomery and his group lost track of him from there."

"So…maybe his van didn't start, and he had to take the bus to work."

"He's not at work. He's usually in by seven," Johnny told her, something she hadn't known. "Mallory opens up at six and Jason is one of the first kids there every morning."

Something else she hadn't known.

Oh, God. Jackson…

"He found out he was being watched," she said, feeling lightheaded.

"We don't know that yet." Johnny's voice was close, reassuring. His arm came around her, and he led her to the couch.

She *needed* to know. And had to pull it together. She wasn't some weak-kneed woman who couldn't be there for her son.

Except that she hadn't been. She'd dropped him off and driven away, leaving Mark to pack him up and run…

She looked at Johnny. Focused on the encouragement in his blue eyes. He seemed to be promising her something. Panic receded for a second, and she tried to rally her thoughts. Control them. Think.

"What day is it today?"

He said the date and, hearing it aloud, it hit her.

She should've known. "It's the anniversary of his mother's death," she said. The police had given her the date when they'd figured it for the trigger that had set Mark in motion.

"What if he's going to the cemetery?" she said, staring at Johnny. Pulling his phone out of his pocket, he hit a button and was speaking almost immediately. He gave instructions for Alistair to go to the cemetery in Mission Viejo and then had her call Detective Bentley, who said that while they'd kept watch on the grave over the year, they, of course, couldn't have someone there twenty-four/seven. He told her not to get her hopes up, but that they'd send someone over to keep an eye on Mark's mother's plot. They didn't really expect him to just walk up to it right out in the open, though. Not while being on the run.

"If Matt's not Mark, why would he go to the trouble of leaving his home covertly, taking a bus instead of just getting in his van and going about his day?"

"Could be they were taking a bus downtown to the zoo."

Could be.

"Or to the airport. Maybe he didn't want to pay for parking."

Sucking in a sharp breath, she asked, "You think they're running?"

"Or going on a planned vacation. We need to think positive and let Montgomery's team do their jobs."

"What if he realized he was being watched? What if he's run again?"

"Positive thoughts, Tabitha."

She nodded. Had to get over to Mark/Matt's house. To be among Jackson/Jason's things. And knew she couldn't. She had no right to be anywhere near the man. Or his son.

Tabitha's color returned when Johnny got Braden Harris on the phone. Montgomery had visited Harris's professional building. He'd seen that Matt's gym was closed. He'd introduced himself to Mallory and asked if Jason was absent that morning. But Johnny wanted more.

Braden trained with Matt several times a week. At the very least, he would know whether or not his personal training sessions had been canceled. And if so, Johnny wanted the reason Braden had been given.

Montgomery could've done that, too, but Johnny needed to do *something*. And he figured Braden Harris would be more likely to talk to him. The man was all about loyalty, and while he and Johnny weren't buds by any means, they'd established a respect for each other.

"Yeah, I knew he was going to be gone today," Braden said, as soon as Johnny explained the reason for his call. "We rescheduled my morning session."

"When did he reschedule?" If it had been this morning... If the change in plan was that sudden...

"At the end of Tuesday's workout. He said he wouldn't be in on Thursday." So the absence was planned. "We're doing an extra session on Monday to make up for it." And now they knew Matt planned to be back.

"Did he say why he was taking the day off?"

Johnny noted Braden's hesitation. Looked at Tabitha on the couch, watching him, and schooled his features as he'd learned to do in moot court during law school.

"Repeating information that was given to you regarding your own schedule will in no way implicate you in anything."

"I understand," Braden said, his tone congenial but brooking no pressure, either. "His explanation was personal, though."

All the more reason Johnny wanted to hear it. "In your Tuesday session, did you ask him anything pertaining to the list we gave you?" They'd only delivered the list late Monday night. And Braden hadn't called with anything since then.

"I did, actually. I asked him if he was a fan of milk or

dark chocolate because the woman before me had left a box for him." Mark only liked milk chocolate.

"And?"

"He said he's a trainer. He doesn't put chocolate in his body."

A nonanswer.

"Anything else?"

Johnny turned his back to Tabitha when there was another silence on the line. He walked to the window overlooking the harbor. And waited.

"This isn't right," Braden finally said. "Some of the things on that list... Any number of people would have affirmative responses."

"And the more there are, the more compelling our suspicions become."

"He used to inline skate."

Johnny remembered that one. Mark had quit skating after being hit by a truck pulling out of a parking lot just as he was on the road, skating by.

"Did he say why?"

"He said he took a hard fall."

Because he'd been hit by a truck? Johnny wanted to ask.

But he didn't say any more. He just continued to wait. He understood the other man's struggle. And he knew that if he were to push at that moment, the phone call would be over.

"I feel like crap doing this," Braden said.

"If we're wrong, and you feel a need, you can tell Matt that you helped us out under duress. A reasonable man is going to understand. And if there's even the slightest chance that we're right..."

"I'm not comfortable invading this guy's privacy, but he took off because it's the anniversary of his wife's death, okay? Said he wanted to spend the day with Jason, having fun, taking him places Jason's mother would've loved, telling him about her. Now just leave the guy alone, would you?"

Johnny couldn't do that. He told Braden so. And ended the call.

"What are the chances that one man's wife and another man's mother die of the same disease on the exact same day?" he muttered to himself. And that both men had a son the exact same age whose names both started with J. He turned back to Tabitha the second he got off the phone.

"Matt took the day off because it's the anniversary of his wife's death?" She was standing now, her mouth open. She hugged her sides and Johnny wanted the arms wrapped around her to be his.

He told her about the inline skating similarity, too, but still wasn't convinced it meant anything. At least, not by itself. Maybe together with all the other similarities…

"If a guy was hit by a truck, wouldn't he just say so?" he asked her.

"Unless he's changing his stories to fit a new identity, while sticking to enough of the truth to prevent making unnecessary mistakes." Tabitha's tone was even. Almost calm.

And she had a point.

"I think you should call Bentley."

Maybe she could have Jackson back by nightfall…

That possibility brought a myriad of emotions Johnny couldn't identify.

"And since he told Braden he's taking the day off because of the anniversary, he probably doesn't know anything about us. He's going to the gravesite and will come right back," Tabitha continued.

He nodded, agreeing that the chances of that were good, wanting the police to believe, as well. Mark might have handed them the opportunity they needed to catch him. Johnny knew he'd rest easier once Montgomery's people had an eye on Mark/Matt again. Which they should soon. If he went to the cemetery, as predicted.

And as Tabitha expected. She'd insisted from the very beginning that Mark wouldn't go far to start his new life. That he'd need to stay close enough to visit his mother.

"The only thing is…" Tabitha's voice trailed off and she frowned.

"What?"

"Why take the bus?" she asked, a look of fear returning to her eyes. "Why not just drive his son in the family van?"

"Because he doesn't want any part of his current identity tied to his previous one," he said. "I'm guessing he'll keep a low profile, probably wear a hat, baggy clothes, maybe a hoodie."

Which was also why he probably wouldn't go to his mother's grave that day. Matt might visit his wife's grave, if there was one. But Mark…

Johnny's mental gears were in full motion. Adrenaline pumped through his veins. Braden had said that Matt was planning to take his son to places his wife would have loved, not to the cemetery.

"Where would Mark's mother love to be?" he asked Tabitha, picking up his tablet to make a list. She'd mentioned that his mother liked ice cream. And flowers. But very little else.

"Mark never talked about his mom. Like I said, I didn't even know he lived with her until after I'd stopped hanging out with him. After that, he mentioned the ice cream thing once, because he let Jackson try some. And the flowers…he'd taken Jackson to a flower shop to pick up some lilies for his mother at Easter. That's how I knew they were her favorite flower. He said so that day."

If they could figure out where Mark might spend the day, if Montgomery could check out flower shops and ice cream parlors in the area where Mark used to live, or even in San Diego. If they could narrow it down…

If they were right, Tabitha really could have her son in her arms before the sun set on that day.

Another surge of emotion hit Johnny at the thought. Stronger this time. Overwhelming for the few seconds it took him to get himself in check.

There were no guarantees here.

Chapter Sixteen

"**D**etective Bentley said that if Mark took Jackson out for the day, to places his mother had loved, then Jackson will at least be safe. That there's no immediate reason to worry…"

Standing beside Johnny in the Angel's Food Bowls truck, Tabitha repeated that for at least the fifth time. She couldn't help it.

And Johnny, bless him, didn't seem to mind.

"I agree with him," he said, also for the fourth or fifth time. And then, as she stepped aside to give him room to pass, he walked right up to her and put his gloved hands on her arms. It was the first time he'd touched her since the night they'd kissed. "I'm serious, Tabitha. If I thought there was something we could be doing, anything, we'd be out there doing it."

"I know." It had been her idea to open the truck. She'd been told by Detective Bentley to go about her day. To keep her phone on her person at all times, just in case, but to…go about her day. He'd also told her, multiple times, that Matt and Jason might really be Matt and Jason. He'd warned her not to do anything foolish.

Johnny had offered to drive her around to every flower

shop, every ice cream store, between San Diego and Mission Viejo. A sweet gesture, but not a practical one. If Mark saw her and ran... She couldn't risk it. Not when they were this close.

"At least Detective Bentley agreed to put in a call to the San Diego police to see about a request for a DNA warrant on Jason."

When she'd asked, based on the slowly building circumstantial evidence with the new revelation of Mark's mother and Matt's wife dying of the same disease on the same day, he'd said he'd try. She couldn't tell if he'd sounded hopeful or was only humoring her. And she didn't really care as long a judge got a look at the request.

Johnny had written the affidavit; he'd said all the areas of probable cause were mentioned.

He'd emailed the completed document to Detective Bentley before they'd left the hotel room.

After nine months of nothing, things were happening. Shaking with the wonder of it all, and with fear that any one of a million things could go wrong, she raised her hands to Johnny's shoulders. Held on. "Mark might figure out that he's being followed. He might run if the police approach him. Jackson could get hurt."

"Positive thoughts, Tabitha," he reminded her. Then bent his head to kiss her.

Tabitha didn't even think about resisting. She wasn't thinking about sex, either. She just knew that Johnny made her feel better than she'd felt in a very, very long time. So she clung to him.

As the day progressed, Johnny prepared bowls. More than a hundred of them. He listened to Tabitha make conversation with people, heard her be considerate, understanding, reassuring and grateful to their customers. How she remained patient he wasn't sure, but suspected that inside she was falling apart.

He watched her all afternoon. No matter how hard he tried, he couldn't stop looking at her. And every time he did, he felt a resurgence of that kick in the gut he'd had earlier, but he didn't get hard once.

He still found her incredibly attractive. That hadn't changed. He just cared more about holding her up than lying down with her that afternoon.

The hours were some of the longest he'd ever known. Sometime after two, Tabitha glanced at him, and he caught a look of desperation in her eyes and motioned her over. Telling the customer at the front of the line that she'd be right back, she was at his side instantly. "Why haven't we heard?"

"If something had happened, we would have," he told her. "If there was any indication that Matt wasn't returning, or anyone had seen him, or the judge ruled on the warrant, we'd have heard."

"I know. You're right." She leaned over, kissed him quickly and went back to her duties.

Johnny had to take a moment before he could get back to his.

The kisses meant nothing. She knew that. Not in the big picture. They were a way to get through the day. A way to feel good so she had the strength to get through the next minute. The next hour. Johnny had kissed her that first time to distract her. And the second time, she'd just needed the feel-good. The connection.

By four o'clock that afternoon, she was ready to go to bed with him. She was going to need something that huge to take her mind off all the people out there who weren't calling them.

Johnny's phone rang just as she had that thought. There'd only been a couple of people in line over the past five minutes or so. She almost dropped the last bowl as she handed it out the window and then turned to watch Johnny.

Montgomery, he mouthed as he answered. Leaving the window, she moved toward him, taking his hand as he held it out to her. He squeezed. She squeezed back. For that day, Johnny was her lifeline. Just for the day.

She could hear a male voice. Couldn't make out any words. Noise from the boulevard on which they were parked, coupled with the sound of the truck's generator, made it impossible to know what was being said.

Johnny listened. He didn't talk for what seemed an inordinately long time.

"Okay. Thanks, man."

Okay, *what*? What was he thanking him for? Her palms were sweating and she felt a bit nauseous.

"Yeah." And then, "Absolutely."

She was staring at Johnny, who seemed to be focusing on their clasped hands. She didn't think she could take much more.

"Yep," he said and then rang off.

Tabitha wasn't sure she wanted to know what he had to tell her when he finally raised his head and she saw the look in his eyes.

"Mark didn't show up at the cemetery," he said. "No one there has seen him since his mother's funeral. No one in the area recognized his picture. And there's no sign of Matt, either. Montgomery's team showed recent pictures to people at the bus stop where he got off, to other bus drivers and at nearby establishments. They've followed every lead they can and…nothing."

"That just means we don't know what Mark's mom loved. He's taken him someplace she loved."

He nodded and looked as though he might say something else. He didn't, but his gaze was intense. "I'm sorry we don't have more."

"So we didn't get him at the cemetery. Maybe they went to some flower place that specializes in lilies. He got that new lily tattoo because they were her favorite flower." She couldn't give up now.

"I want to promise you that we'll find them. Today. And that Matt and Jason are Mark and Jackson." His tone held no hint of promise at all.

She nodded and didn't move away. "I know, Johnny. It's the succeeder in you. But sometimes it's not a matter of being the best at something. Being able to master it. Sometimes you have to believe *before* you see." And while he might hope or think, she didn't feel like he believed.

He studied her for a second, his blue eyes searching. She wanted to give him whatever fact or belief he was missing, but she didn't know what that was. "Sometimes it has to matter enough," she told him. "Whatever you're looking for. Or hoping to achieve."

He tilted his head, as though waiting for more.

She had no more. All she knew was that she believed she'd find her son. Jason, Jackson, whatever they were calling him. That she wouldn't stop until she had him home. And that she was scared to death something would happen to him in the meantime.

"Besides," she said, "we still have Detective Bentley trying to get a DNA warrant. Maybe not today, but possibly by tomorrow."

She prayed to God that Matt didn't run. That after

speaking with Detective Bentley, the San Diego police would take the case seriously and keep him in their sights.

"Montgomery is posting agents at the front and back entrances of Matt's house starting tonight," Johnny told her. The detective had followed the man home one night to get the address.

It was going to cost her Jackson's college fund, the rest of the insurance money she'd received after her mother's accident and probably savings she didn't yet have, but she'd pay him back for the investigator. Somehow.

He lowered his head. He was going to kiss her again. She wanted him to.

"Excuse me! Anyone in there?" a voice called.

Tabitha jerked back, hurried to the window and took care of the customer. Maybe it was for the best that she and Johnny had stopped playing with a fire that would eventually incinerate her.

Johnny stood in the shower Thursday evening, his mind busy. *Sometimes it has to matter enough.* Tabitha's words played and replayed, looking for a place to land, finding none. She'd hit on the flaw that had plagued him all his life. Nothing mattered enough.

Things mattered. But not enough to ignite the kind of passion that drove a man to make certain choices simply because he had to. She'd said that sometimes you have to believe before you see, but he'd never needed to do that. Exactly the opposite. He saw, believed he could make it happen and then did. Whether it was mastery of a sport or a musical instrument, receiving a college degree, closing a deal or winning a case. Even with Angel…he'd seen the woman who was right for him, one he'd loved casually most of his life. He'd seen his parents' relationship and set out to make his own marriage work.

And now...he saw Tabitha's need to have her son back in her arms, in her life. But he couldn't seem to make it happen for her. The defeat was crushing him.

So he'd just keep trying, like his father had said. As long as he tried, there was a possibility of success. Maybe not with Matt and Jason. Maybe not in San Diego. But Mark and Jackson had to be *somewhere*. Thinking that if things in San Diego didn't pan out, he'd hire Montgomery and his team to handle Jackson's case overall. To turn every stone to find the child. Tabitha would never be able to afford the cost.

Perhaps he'd start a nonprofit to find missing children and use the proceeds from Angel's Food Bowls to finance it. Jackson would be their first case...

Pleased with where his mind was taking him, Johnny finished his shower, eager to meet Tabitha out in the suite for the Italian feast they'd ordered from room service, which should be arriving in a few minutes. They still had three more nights and four days left of the trip. Anything could happen in that time.

The warrant could come through in the morning. By tomorrow night, Tabitha could have Jackson safely in her arms—or at least the DNA testing might be in process. He knew a guy who knew a guy and had the ability to pay the lab enough extra to get almost immediate results.

In the meantime, he'd support the heck out of her. Fulfilling his promises to their partnership. He'd been keeping his distance since their near miss on the couch the other night. Or, rather, their foray into erotically incredible territory. He wasn't even sure anymore why he'd pulled so far back from her.

Or let her pull back from him without noticing. But seeing her that morning, about to fall when she thought there was bad news about her son...watching her hold herself up all day…finding a strength he'd never seen displayed in one individual before, he'd been unable to stand back any longer.

Tabitha shouldn't be alone. No one deserved to go through tragedy alone. She was in the middle of her second and still standing. And he was there, the one she'd invited in.

Why him? He had no idea. Why no one else in all the years since her mother had been killed in that accident, he couldn't say.

But she'd seen something in Johnny, something he sure as hell didn't see in himself, and he'd be damned if he was going to let her down.

Didn't matter that there were limits on their time together. That their partnership would dissolve. What mattered was she'd asked someone—him—to share her load for a while and he was going to succeed at doing so.

Just as she'd helped him succeed with Angel's Food Bowls. They'd made a deal and he always kept up his end of any deal.

Checking his phone as he headed out to the suite's living room, he saw a missed call from Montgomery. A voice mail. And Tabitha, in sweats and a long-sleeved cotton shirt like she'd worn at home during their list-making nights. Barefoot, like him, she was sitting with her legs curled up under her on the couch.

"Dinner hasn't arrived yet," she told him, looking more relaxed than she had all day.

"Montgomery called," he said, hating to bring tension back into the room. He was listening to the voice mail by the time he reached her.

"What?" She didn't even let him move the phone away from his ear before she was on him.

"Matt and Jason got home, on foot, about half an hour

ago. Jason was carrying a stuffed toy and Matt had one like it, several sizes larger. They were both wearing San Diego Zoo hats."

"They went to the zoo?"

"You know anything about Mark's mother being fond of animals?"

She shook her head. "But like I said, I know almost nothing about her. I don't even know if he had a pet growing up."

She had to be able to depend on him, at the very least. "Maybe she liked the zoo," he said anyway, giving her hope.

Because she had to believe before she'd see and she most definitely needed to see her son again. If it turned out that Jackson wasn't this boy, he'd help her look at photos until there was another. She had a small smile on her face. A sad one.

"You doing okay?" he asked.

"Yeah." Picking up the pillow he'd held over his lap the other night, she hugged it to her. "At least I know they're home safely. That Matt really was bringing Jason back. And tomorrow, when the warrant comes through…"

"If it comes through…" He could encourage, but he couldn't lead her on.

"Can we just not worry about that tonight?"

Room service knocked at the door before he had a chance to answer her.

Chapter Seventeen

"I've missed you the past couple of days, Johnny." Tabitha held a breadstick, munching on it as she walked around the suite. Touching things. Pulling out drawers. She'd already wheeled their dinner cart out into the hall, leaving what was left of the basket of breadsticks on the table.

"I've been right here." Johnny was still at the table for two in front of the windows, sipping from the glass of wine he'd ordered with dinner. Hers was half empty on the table across from him.

She'd eaten some of her dinner—more than she'd expected to—but she'd been restless, finding various reasons to get up from the table. She'd needed a tissue. Had gone to turn down the thermostat, thinking it was a little hot in the room. She just couldn't seem to sit still.

Now she wanted to do something so completely out of character she wasn't sure she actually could.

"Your body's been here," she told him. "My partner's been here. But ever since we kissed, you've been acting like I'm a leper."

"I kissed you three times today. I have to say I don't think I'd ever kiss a leper." Exactly. Those kisses—gentle and sweet though they'd been—were prompting her to act like a crazy woman. She knew it but couldn't find any desire to stop. On the contrary. If she didn't get under Johnny's skin a little bit, she might just fly out of hers before the night was through.

And before they got to morning—and, she hoped, the judge's decision. By noon she might have Jackson's DNA. If they got the warrant, Johnny would pay the lab to rush the results, and with hers as the other sample, a determination should be pretty easy.

They'd talked about the process all the way through closing the truck down for the night.

She didn't want to think about labs and judges sitting on their benches making rulings that affected people for the rest of their lives. Didn't want to picture the person who, in the morning, might hold her future in his or her hands.

And she didn't want to worry about Mark running once he knew the jig was up. It wasn't like the DNA authorization would include a warrant for Mark's arrest. Until the test came back, he was Matt, father of Jason, not Mark, kidnapper of Tabitha's baby boy.

Sliding back onto her seat, she picked up her glass of wine then glanced out at the harbor. She saw a reflection of the room's light in the glass. Jumping up, she turned off most of the lights in the living room portion of the suite. "There, now the view is nicer," she said.

Slouched in his chair, looking satiated and comfortable, Johnny narrowed his eyes as he stared across at her and said, "Yes, it is."

She'd meant the harbor view.

She looked out to sea. Thought about all the people who died before they'd done everything they wanted to do. People like her mother. Like Angel. And not everyone had a Johnny who'd take on what was left undone.

Sipping her wine, she could practically feel the heat emanating from her companion.

Her Johnny. Not the one who'd grown up with wealth, who had wealth, who would return to wealth.

For this time, for the next few days, maybe even the next couple of months, Johnny was her partner.

Her companion.

Whether he knew it or not, he was the best friend she'd ever had.

"I've been thinking about your problem," she said. The words had sounded better in the shower than they did out here in the open.

"What problem?"

He was supposed to have gotten it right away. She'd pictured this playing out with a sexy smirk on his face.

"The one we talked about the other night."

He frowned. "Listen, Tabitha, we don't have to let that get in the way. I'm sorry I was…distant the past couple of days, but I'm over it. I'm here for you. I've always been here. And I'm not going anywhere. I swear to you."

"I was hoping you'd go to bed with me tonight."

Wow. The power of those words almost knocked her off her seat. Way more out there than they'd seemed in the shower.

He wasn't saying a word. Just tapping his finger against the stem of his wineglass. She'd thought he'd be taking her hand, leading her to his room. Or hers. Even the couch would be better than sitting there across from him.

Then he smiled. A weird kind of smile. One she'd never seen on him before. And yet…still all Johnny. "I appreciate the offer." His tone was kind. Congenial. "And you have to realize I'm tempted. But…no."

Cold now, she wished she hadn't turned down the heat. Nowhere in her imaginings of this moment had she seen a rejection coming. "Why not?"

She wasn't sure she wanted to know. But she didn't know how to extricate herself, either.

"You had sex with Mark out of grief over the loss of a patient."

She'd forgotten he knew that. But…yeah. "I don't get your point."

"Sex is for enjoyment between two people who want it equally."

"You want it with me. You made that pretty obvious."

"I'm not denying that."

"And I want it."

"I don't think you do."

If she wasn't feeling so…strange, she might start to feel angry, instead. "You think I don't know what I want?"

"I think you're the sweetest woman I've ever met, the most nurturing, and you're trying to be a good friend to me because I'm helping you through a tough time."

She took a minute to consider what he'd said. *Was* that what she was doing?

"No, that's not it." She shook her head.

"You're going to tell me and expect me to believe that you've developed a sudden passion for my body during the past two days?"

Maybe. His kiss a few nights ago had changed her. "I've never felt…huge passion in that area…"

He stopped tapping on his glass. He studied her intently, then lifted his wine to take a long sip.

"I've been too busy taking care of myself, watching

out for all the roadblocks because I knew there wasn't anyone who'd be there to pick me up if I fell..." She didn't want him to think she was undersexed.

Even if she was.

"You've never been so racked with passion that you just couldn't say no? Couldn't stop?"

"No."

"Then why have sex?"

"When I was younger...because it was kind of expected, I guess." Even to her, the reasoning sounded lame.

"And later?"

"There was only Mark. That one time." She couldn't imagine that any of this was helping her cause. If he'd been turned on, been picturing her as this sexy woman who'd fulfill his needs, she was disappointing him.

"Because you were grieving."

She didn't want to think about Mark. About that night. And how it might, just a little, mirror this one. "Sometimes you need the ultimate human contact, you know? You need to connect. To feel that you're fully alive and part of something outside your own small world."

He lifted his glass again. Drank. Watched her the whole time.

"And that's what you need now? This ultimate human contact?"

She could nod. See where it led them. "I need you to hold me, Johnny." She let the truth fall out. "When you kissed me today, it was like...I knew I could hang on for another hour. I've got eight hours of darkness to get through here. I don't want to do it alone."

"So I'll hold you. All night long. You don't have to have sex to get my arms around you, hon. You only had to ask."

Hon.

The word sent a shiver of…something even better than his kiss arcing through her. She wanted to be his hon.

"And if I want to make love with you?"

"Let's cross that bridge when we come to it. *If* we come to it."

He stood. Held out his hand. Tabitha took it. Pretty sure they were about to come to that bridge.

What should he wear? Used to sleeping in the buff, or on rare occasions his boxers, Johnny wasn't sure it was a good idea to climb into bed with Tabitha with just a layer of thin fabric between his overactive body part and her…body.

He could always lie there in his jeans. It wasn't as though he'd be getting much sleep. Not in bed with Tabitha. The plan was to help her through the night. To help her get the rest she needed. Whether the judge's decision came in the morning and whether it was in their favor or not, she had a tough day ahead of her tomorrow.

Should he take her to her room? Or his? One way or the other, he expected to be up most of the night and might need his tablet…or other stuff…so he started toward his room with Tabitha following. Then he thought about the fact that she might be more comfortable in hers.

"Is this okay?" he asked. She was the one who'd be asleep all night. Wouldn't even know what room she was in.

"Of course," she told him. He felt her shiver. He wished it was with anticipation and knew he needed to get her under the covers and warm her up.

"We can turn the TV on," he said before they'd reached his door. She'd said once that she fell asleep to the TV most nights. She'd mentioned it months ago, when they'd been talking about a show they'd both watched late the night before.

"Okay."

Good, then. They had a plan.

"Aren't you getting under the covers with me?" Tabitha peered at him from his bed. He was standing by it, TV remote in hand. She'd climbed in, sweats and all, when he'd pulled back the covers.

"Yeah, sure," he said. There was no way he could lie under that blanket with jeans on all night long. He'd bake them both out of the bed.

But jeans would keep his penis contained, no matter what it decided to do.

He found a movie for them to watch—a comedy with very little romance—and tossed the remote on the bed.

"You want your wine?" It might help her fall asleep faster.

"Okay."

He didn't run from the room, but he would've liked to. He brought their glasses and the bottle, too. For her. All for her. Until she passed out on him.

She was propped up on pillows when he got back. Two more were arranged beside her. Close beside her. Made sense, since the idea was for him to hold her. A difficult thing to do from the far side of the bed. Johnny handed Tabitha her glass. Set his and the bottle down on the nightstand. Turned off the lights.

Jeans or boxers. Jeans or boxers.

He pulled his shirt off.

Jeans or boxers.

The only light in the room came from the TV.

He stepped out of his jeans.

* * *

If she'd asked herself about lying in bed with Johnny, watching TV, Tabitha might have figured it would be awkward. She might have been uncomfortable. In reality, she lay there wishing he'd look at her instead of the TV.

She gave him his glass of wine. Sipped from hers. Wondered when he'd get to the holding her part.

So she could reach that bridge she wanted to cross.

Ten minutes went by. Fifteen. And she'd had about as much as she could take. Putting her glass down on the table, she took his from him and looking him straight in the eye, but not saying a word, slid on top of him.

Strange, really, how easy it was. Her body on his, fitting against his, as though it was the most natural thing in the world.

"Have we crossed it yet?" she asked him, driven by feelings in her groin, her breasts, her most private parts. Feelings that weren't going to be told *no*.

"Crossed what?" His strangled-sounding words made her smile.

She'd never seen herself as a seductress. Or even as the aggressor in a physical situation. But she was pushed to her limit. And reaching the end of her time with Johnny.

"The bridge," she said, sliding her pelvis against his completely, gloriously engorged penis. Might have been better for him if she'd been wearing silk instead of sweats.

"Oh, sweetheart, I think you crossed that the second you climbed into my bed," he said, rolling her over and lying on top of her. "I can hold you all night if you want to go outside and sit by a tree." He growled as he lowered his head to her lips.

Johnny didn't start out slow. He didn't ease her into the world of passion. He opened his mouth over hers and used his tongue to send signals all over her body.

Their clothes were gone almost immediately, but that felt natural, too, being naked with Johnny. She couldn't see much with only the TV's glow, not nearly enough, and still couldn't stop looking at him.

She loved how he stared at her. Took moments to devour every part of her with his mouth as he removed her sweats and shirt, her panties and bra, piece by piece.

He touched her in places that shouldn't make her wet down below, but did. He made love to every part of her, and let her make love to every part of him, too, when the urge became more than she could resist.

And when, after what seemed like hours of being on the verge of exploding right out of her body, he grabbed a condom from his wallet and finally spread her legs with his knee and slipped inside her, she cried out, feeling a pleasure she'd never even imagined.

She didn't care that he was only on loan. Didn't worry about losing him. She just gave him everything she had, took everything he wanted to give, thankful that, right now, Johnny was all hers.

Chapter Eighteen

Waking up alone Friday morning, Johnny went about his usual business. Tabitha always had coffee going in the suite by the time he got up and that morning was no different. Standing there in his boxers, he poured himself a cup, looking toward her closed bedroom door.

How long had she lain with him? He remembered waking up at some point with her snuggled against him. And then…nothing.

Her decision to leave his bed before they saw each other again had probably been a good one. No awkward moments.

Still, it might have been nice to wake up together.

If they were in another place and time. If their worlds coincided on a more permanent basis.

The closed door bothered him. He considered knocking on it, but didn't. They had a truck to run. A business to tend to. A partnership still in effect.

Heading toward the shower, he thought about the truck. About the people he was going to contact to get the franchising in motion. Investors he knew he could count on. Angel would have been thrilled.

That was when it hit him. He'd just made love for the first time since his wife's death.

As the water poured onto his head, he waited for guilt to rain down on him, as well. For recrimination to strike. When it didn't come immediately he grabbed the soap. The washcloth. Remembered the incredible sex he'd had with Tabitha. Relived the way he'd felt—and not just physically. He waited to hate himself for it. Still nothing.

Except a peculiar warmth he felt from the inside out. Go figure.

Tabitha kissed Johnny four times that morning. Not passionate, get-naked kisses, just check-in kisses. Grounding her wires so she didn't short-circuit. The first time had been when they were standing at the door of their suite, ready to leave. They'd met in the living room, in their Angel's Food Bowls garb, as always. She'd worried that it might be awkward. That he might want to talk about what they'd done. That she might be embarrassed.

He'd been as great, as always. Normal. With an extra-warm look thrown in. That was when she'd kissed him. And thanked him.

He didn't ask what for.

She didn't elaborate—even to herself.

The second time had been right before they opened the window on the truck for business. He'd brushed by her, stopping to press his body against hers just for a second.

The third had been a quickie when they had a moment with no customers.

And the fourth... That had happened when she'd glanced at her watch, seen that noon had arrived and realized they still hadn't heard from the judge. They'd obviously missed his or her morning calendar. There were five customers in line, all wanting things from her, and it was just too much. Her chest had tightened. Drawing in air had been a struggle. And she'd walked over and kissed Johnny while his hands were covered with meat and lettuce. Because connecting with him made her stronger.

The fact that he didn't seem to object, no matter how many times they kissed, made it fun. A moment of levity at a grave time.

By two that afternoon, she needed more than a kiss. More than any momentary relief from the tension. Still no word from the judge. No word from anyone.

Matt was back at work and Jason was back at the daycare. If they hadn't been, Alistair Montgomery would have called. She and Johnny were running the food truck. Neither Mallory nor Braden seemed to be making much use of her list. Other than Johnny's call to Braden the day before, there'd been no contact with the Harrises.

And she'd had sex with her partner. Her friend.

That morning, their actions hadn't bothered her all that much. Maybe she'd still been on an endorphin high or something. But as the day waned, as the evening loomed, she started to think about the night ahead.

Would she and Johnny go to their own rooms as normally as they'd come out of them this morning? Would they have dinner out first, so there was no temptation to sleep together again?

She had some say in the matter. A *lot* of say. She just had no idea *what* to say. In a perfect world, she'd sleep with him again, but her world was far from perfect and—

Her phone rang.

A jolt shot through her, increasing her heart rate and slowing her breath. Tabitha excused herself from the window, moved closer to Johnny and pulled her phone from her pocket.

"It's Detective Bentley," she said softly and then, tapping to answer, spoke into the phone. "Hello?"

The detective introduced himself and she knew the news wasn't good from his tone of voice. They'd spoken that often. She could tell.

"The judge denied our request," he told her. "She said the evidence wasn't compelling enough to impinge on the privacy of a citizen who, other than his similarities to another man, had no indicators of having committed a crime. She wanted some evidence that proved Matt could be suspected of wrongdoing. I'm so sorry, Ms. Jones. I wish I could do more, but…"

Tabitha got through the phone call. She managed some kind of thank-you and a proper goodbye.

"We didn't get the warrant," she told Johnny, and then went back to work.

She would go on. She could go on.

She had to go on.

Jackson was still out there. Waiting.

Johnny suggested dinner at the beach, followed by a walk on the sand. He wanted romance, but didn't expect it. Wasn't actually convinced it was a good idea. His time with Tabitha was coming to an end, and even though he fully intended to stay in touch with her, to answer if she ever called him. To be there if she ever needed him. He knew she'd been right when she said that once he returned home his life would consume him.

Just as hers would consume her if she got her son back.

He also knew he couldn't delay his own life until that point. It could be years. Or never.

Still, he couldn't pretend the night before had never happened. They'd had fantastic sex. Even if they weren't going to do it again, that was worth acknowledging.

Taking heart from her ready agreement with his suggestion that they stay down at the beach for the evening, Johnny took her to a seafood place with balcony seating over the sand. Ordered them both a glass of wine. Over dinner he talked to her about his Angel's Food Bowls franchise plan—including the use of the proceeds to fund a nonprofit that aided parents in the search for missing children.

"To give you an idea of how that could look," he said, "parents could apply for money to fund a private investigator…"

Her smile was so personal, Johnny felt like he'd just closed the deal. Except that there wasn't a deal on the table. Yet.

"That sounds wonderful, Johnny," she said. And something occurred to him, right there on the spot.

"I was thinking you could hold a position on the board," he said. "Of the nonprofit. Like maybe head it up."

He wanted romance and he was offering her a *job*?

Her glow continued to warm him. "I would love that, Johnny. Seriously. I don't know how much time it would take, but I'll find the time. I think it's a great idea."

He honestly didn't know how much time it would take, either. He was working on the fly here, which was so unheard of for him, he wasn't sure what came next.

"You'll get a salary," he told her. Because he knew that much. Knew quite a bit, actually. He just hadn't made any spreadsheets yet for this particular project. He had to have a budget, to estimate his profits per franchise per year, put out feelers to get an idea of how many franchises they could expect to sell in the first year, and at what fees. There'd be permits and licensing costs. The nonprofit would need startup and marketing budgets—

"You don't have to pay me, Johnny. I'm happy to do whatever I can…" Tabitha interrupted his thoughts. And spawned new ones. If she was running the nonprofit, he could keep in touch with her. Even if just peripherally.

"Wait until you find out the workload before you say that," he said. If the food truck franchising didn't produce enough income, he could talk to his father; there were other monies they could donate to the nonprofit. This thing was going to roll. It had to. And Tabitha… she was enthusiastic about it. As he'd known she would be. Yeah, she had to run it.

And if he got to work immediately, the nonprofit could be ready to go before his sabbatical was over. Adrenaline pumped through him. He was going to make it happen.

She was smiling at him.

"What?" he asked.

"You're full of energy all of a sudden…"

He was.

"I'm just not used to it. Usually you're more laid-back… I guess I'm getting a glimpse of Johnny the corporate attorney."

No, he was pretty laid-back all the time. Didn't get wound up about much, which was part of what made him good at what he did—whatever he did. He didn't clog anything up with emotional baggage.

And if Tabitha was going to be working for him, they really needed to clear up the sex thing.

Paying their bill, he suggested they take a walk. The ocean air would be balmy. Fresh air was a must at the moment.

He started right in as soon as they were on the sand. "We need to talk about last night."

"I was kind of hoping we wouldn't."

"It's there."

"I know. I didn't say I didn't think we needed to. I said I was hoping we wouldn't."

"So…you agree? We need to address it."

"Okay."

He took a couple more steps, shoving his hands in the pockets of his jeans instead of reaching for her hand. He'd established the purpose of this meeting. The walk. Made it clear.

And didn't like what he had to deal with.

"It's okay, Johnny. You needn't worry that I'll make any more out of it than it was, if that's what's bothering you."

Good to know, but he wasn't sure that was it.

"I knew the score going in," she said. "We've got another couple of months together, max, and then the partnership dissolves."

He wasn't even sure what that meant anymore.

"We'll be forming a new partnership, of sorts," he was quick to point out. "With the nonprofit."

"I hope you get it up and running," she told him. "I really do think it's a wonderful idea and I'd be excited to help out in any way I can," she said. He heard a "but" in her tone. Didn't ask about it.

"All I'm saying," she continued when he still didn't take back control of the meeting he'd instigated, "is that you aren't going to be living next door to me. Or be anywhere in my sphere. We live two completely different lives, and I just want you to know I won't be hounding you or going to the press or…even telling anyone I once knew you. Like I said, I won't make more of this than there was."

What if *he* wanted to make more of it? The thought occurred and he figured it was coming more from his crotch than his brain.

His brain told him, however, that she was right on all counts.

"Besides, I can hardly blame *you* for what happened or try to trap you into something when I'm the one who came on to you."

He hadn't missed that point. Had revisited it numerous times over the past hours. Always with a hard-on.

"It was…unlike you," he said.

"I know."

"Probably because of the wine." And because he'd made his physical need for her such a big deal earlier in the week. That hadn't been the fairest move. Not when he knew she was relying on him more than usual with all the Jason stuff going on.

"It wasn't the wine, Johnny." She didn't miss a step. "I made the choice before you even opened the bottle."

"You aren't keen on unconditional sex," he reminded her. "And clearly don't take sex lightly, based on the fact that you've only had one lover in years."

"Two, now."

Her statement, the droll tone of her voice, went straight to his groin.

Two, now. Yes, he was now one of her lovers. That put a little extra oomph in his step.

"And you're right," she continued. "I don't take sex lightly. I didn't take last night lightly. I just don't want you to think I have any intention of cashing in on what happened. You're an incredibly rich man. I've only just begun to realize how rich." Her chuckle sounded a bit uncomfortable. "Much richer than I realized."

Okay, he got the *rich* part. The way she kept saying the word made him feel like he should go take a shower, rid himself of some of his richness.

Her tone was respectful. The words were, too. There

was also the implication that the richer he got, the farther away from her he'd be.

"I'm sure you've had women using you, hoping to get something out of you, and I want to assure you that's not me."

She wasn't trying to get something out of him. And she wasn't looking for more.

"Why, then?" he asked. He lost all desire for sex as a thought occurred to him. "Tell me you didn't have sex with me to put me out of my misery. As some kind of mercy act. Or a way to pay me back for helping you out." The words alone, saying them, made him feel sick to his stomach.

"Of course not!" She took his hand. Squeezed it. "I wanted it as badly as you did."

Okay, things were looking up again. "Physically?" He wasn't taking anything for granted.

"Yes. You're… Last night was… I had no idea it could be like that."

"So, you want to do it again?"

"Yeaahh…"

"But?"

"Is it the best choice, knowing our partnership's going to end soon?"

He couldn't answer that.

For either of them.

Chapter Nineteen

On and off all day, ever since Detective Bentley's call, Tabitha had been fighting panic. The kind she'd felt right after her mother had been killed and she'd known she was all alone in the world and had no idea how she'd survive.

And again the day Jackson was kidnapped.

Could it be possible that she'd found her son and still had no way to get him back?

And yet, anytime she came close to the point of needing to lie down in a corner in the fetal position until her strength came back, she'd turn to Johnny and she'd find her power.

Which brought its own kind of worry. She knew she'd be fine when he was gone. Just as she'd survived the loss of the two people she'd loved most in the world.

She'd go to work, distract herself from her own pain by focusing on little ones who were feeling a pain she could hardly imagine. The children at work gave her more strength than they'd ever know. Helping them helped her.

But they weren't on the Jackson quest. Work wasn't part of that. Only Johnny was.

She'd asked him if it was wrong to spend a second

night in each other's arms when they both knew their current relationship was going to end.

He hadn't answered.

"What if I'm using you, Johnny, just not for your money?"

"What on earth does that mean? Using me how? You said you were turned on and so was I. It was mutual."

"I *was* turned on!" Boy, was she. More than she'd ever figured. "I still am!" Who would think, after the night she'd shared with Johnny, that she'd be more turned on than she'd been in her life? That she needed him more tonight than she had the night before?

"So?" He shrugged. While she was glad of the darkness at the beach and the lack of other walkers that late at night in September, she wished she could see his face.

Wished she knew where she was going with this whole conversation.

"Being with you makes me feel…more capable of handling the challenges I'm facing," she said slowly, thinking about every word to make certain she was getting them completely right. "When I touch you, it brings good feelings. So when the bad feelings start to overwhelm me, I touch you and get a moment's relief. But I know it's only while we're going through this time together. I mean, I know I'll face my future challenges without leaning on you."

He stopped walking. Turned her to face him. The light of the moon left a white streak on one side of his face. The other was in complete darkness.

"What are you trying to say? Because I have to tell you, I'm not getting it."

She wasn't sure she was, either. She just needed him to know that when the partnership ended, it ended. Needed him to know she understood that.

"I want to make sure you're okay with my leaning on you for now."

"Isn't that what our partnership is all about?"

That was true, of course. So she kissed him.

It was the only answer she had.

And, based on the way he pulled her against him, she figured it was the right one.

Johnny liked sex. Was good at it. He knew how to please a woman and enjoyed doing so. And when it was done, he was fine to move on to sleep. Television. A nightcap. A shower.

He made love to Tabitha that night, and when it was done, he wanted more. Apparently so did she, because when he pushed back the covers to expose her breast and then leaned in to take her nipple into his mouth, she arched and asked for more. Eventually he had to take a break. Let her have a break, too. TV still didn't beckon. Nor did sleep, a drink or a shower.

He wanted more of *her*. More than just her body. He wanted to give her something that would see her through however many months or years it took to get her son back in her life.

She wasn't going to fail. Because she was never going to quit trying.

And, as it turned out, he hadn't failed, either. He had a plan to help her, and others like her, in the future, with the added bonus of keeping her in his life.

Until her son was found, he'd continue to help. To pay Montgomery.

In the nearly ten years since her mother's death, she'd been a loner. Hadn't let anyone inside her life far enough to help her. She'd let him in.

Nope, he wasn't going to fail her.

But…

"Why me?" With his head on his pillow, her head on his shoulder, he wasn't even sure she was still awake until she looked at him.

"What?"

"Your whole adult life, since your mother was killed, it sounds like you've handled everything on your own."

"Yeah." She spoke as if it was a no big deal. "What choice did I have?"

"I'm sure there were people along the way who would've been glad to help."

Her pause was significant. He wanted to know what she was thinking. Who she might be remembering. Wanted to know all her stories.

"I guess there were," she finally said, slowly. "But they didn't *have* to help."

"That doesn't mean they didn't want to."

"I know."

"So?"

He felt her sigh. Settled her more securely against him.

"When my mom died, that feeling…you know, of being all alone in the world…I had to handle it or die. I handled it."

He frowned. "What are you saying? You plan to be alone for the rest of your life so you don't get hurt again?"

"No." She didn't sound sure. "I just… Your parents, they have to love you, help you. At least, in the normal scheme of things. Losing that, not having any other family to step in…there's no one who *has* to help me. So I help myself."

"But what if they *want* to help you?"

He couldn't be the only one who'd wanted that. She was too kind, too giving, to be overlooked by other people like her.

"I… It's better for me to do it myself."

"Why?"

"Because." She was getting testy. He should drop it.

"Why?" he asked for the second time.

"Because I know I won't let me down."

"You're afraid."

"No, I'm not." Maybe she didn't think she was.

"Seems like you are. Afraid of loving and losing again." He was pushing her away, and yet he couldn't stop. Something bigger than lying in bed with her was going on.

"Well, can you blame me? I couldn't even hold on to my own son." She sat up, taking the covers with her to hold against her breasts as she grabbed her shirt. He let her go. Didn't try to stop her from leaving the bed, dressing. Didn't try to follow her, either.

"Just answer my original question," he said, propped up against all four pillows as she scooped up the underthings she hadn't bothered to put on and moved toward the door. "Why me?"

"Because from the very beginning, you were never going to last. I knew that our partnership would be dissolving," she blurted, reaching for the door handle. "I knew what not to expect."

"Tabitha!" He was up now, too. Stepping into his jeans.

"What?" Her back was to him, but she'd stopped.

"What if I don't want the partnership to dissolve?" What was he saying? Of course it had to dissolve! "Or… what if I want a new partnership with you? One where we keep in touch. One with the nonprofit as a project we take on together?"

"We'd be in touch for business, maybe. I'm not going to need anything else. Jackson is at The Bouncing Ball. Somehow I'm going to get him home."

But she was coming back toward the bed.

It occurred to him then that she was going to need him to hold her up if that boy turned out to be a two-year-old who'd been named Jason at birth. He had to do whatever it took to persuade her to let him hold her up.

"You know what I meant," he said. "I'll be around."

Dropping down to the edge of the bed, she clasped her hands, brushing her thumbs back and forth over her palms. He sat beside her, taking her hands in his.

"I wish you'd give me a chance to be a friend who hangs around," he said, feeling like he was fighting the case of his life.

"I'm not pushing you out of my life, Johnny, although I guess it might seem that way. I'm right here, in the partnership, until you're ready to resume your life. We had a setback with the warrant rejection, but we've still got Mallory and Braden watching for any signs, they have the lists, Alistair's still watching Matt. At some point we're going to find evidence compelling enough to get a warrant.

"And I'm truly thrilled at the idea of working on the nonprofit. I keep thinking about it, and it's such a great idea. But beyond that, I have to be realistic. When you're here, living in my world, in the little house next door to me, we have a lot in common. But when you're back in your real life, we probably won't have anything in common at all. You'll be flying corporate jets and…I'm still going to be here. The truth is I *am* going to be alone."

He couldn't argue with her logic.

"Do you mind if I hold you tonight, at least? Or maybe for the next couple of nights? Until we get home?"

"I don't mind." She took her clothes back off as he removed his. Climbed back into bed with him. But he was pretty sure, as she laid her head on his chest, that there'd been a sheen of tears in her eyes.

Chapter Twenty

Saturday was a busy day on the food truck. They opened at ten in the morning, a couple of hours earlier than usual, and had a crowd almost from the beginning. Tabitha was glad of the business. Eager to talk to people, to see them out together, happy, living normal lives.

And she was glad to have Johnny there in the truck with her. Too busy to engage in conversation, but still close.

Surprisingly, they'd been fine waking up together that morning. They'd showered in their own rooms, but with the doors open, and met up to leave as if they'd been living together for months.

Several times that morning, she'd wondered about staying together once they got back to Mission Viejo. Just until it was time for him to go.

She could see the dangers. The pitfalls. The longer she slept with him, the closer she'd feel and the harder it would be to lose him.

But now that she knew she wouldn't be losing all contact, she saw less harm in having as much of him as she could during the time they had left. She wasn't going to stop living because she was afraid of being hurt.

His statement to that effect had really hurt.

She was at the point of running various scenarios through her mind, trying to come up with ways to broach the topic with Johnny, when she noticed the police car parking across the street from their truck. A uniformed officer got out. Came toward the truck.

She glanced at Johnny. And then she realized the man probably just wanted a bowl for lunch. Word was getting around about them.

There were four people in line ahead of him, but the officer didn't wait. He went straight to the window.

"Are you Ms. Tabitha Jones?" he asked. His blond hair and blue eyes made him look…kind. His bulk was a little intimidating.

"Yes." Her mind was blank just then.

"Tabitha?" Johnny must have seen, or heard, the officer because he was behind her.

"I need to speak with you, ma'am," the officer said. "If you could please come with me?"

Heart pounding, she glanced at Johnny again. *She* was in trouble?

"I'm sorry, we're going to have to close," Johnny was saying to the people gathering around the truck. He gave no explanation. Just exited the truck as she got her purse, then closed and locked up the window and the truck. Keys in one hand, he grabbed her hand with the other.

The officer led them to his car.

"What's this about?" Johnny asked, stopping a couple of feet short of the car.

The man looked at Tabitha. "I believe we have your son, ma'am. I was sent to bring you to the station to be reunited with him."

Tabitha's tears were instantaneous and uncontrollable. She had no questions. She was aware of nothing but the open car door. Sliding inside. Hearing white noise in her head. Seeing flashes of color, of bodies milling around. The car started and began to move.

Johnny sat in the back of the patrol car, watching Tabitha, who'd been shown to the front seat, willing her to turn around. She didn't.

Nor did she speak. Not to the officer, who'd said detectives would explain things to her at the station, and not to Johnny. She sat still, although periodically she reached up to wipe her face. It was as though she was afraid to believe Jackson was really at the end of the car ride. Afraid to believe her wait was almost over.

She'd done what he suspected was all she knew how to do anymore—closed in to take care of herself.

The second the car stopped at the station, she was out of it. Moving toward the door. Johnny caught up with her. "Maybe we should wait for the officer," he suggested.

She jumped as if she hadn't even known he was there. But she nodded. Stopped. Stared at the door.

They were shown down a long hall and into a small conference room where they were told to wait. Tabitha hugged herself, standing right in front of the door, and it was too difficult to watch.

"Hey," Johnny said, putting his arms around her. "It's going to be good." What the hell he meant by that, he had no idea. He just had to let her know she wasn't alone.

The door opened and she gasped. And then grew still. A woman in a brown suit stood there, but there was no child.

"I'm Detective Shanley," she said, holding out her hand. "I've been working with Detective Bentley in Mission Viejo and just need to speak with you for a few minutes."

"Where's Jackson?" Tabitha asked. "Is he okay?"

"He's fine," the detective assured her, guiding them to a thin-cushioned couch with metal arms in a corner of the room. As soon as they were seated, Johnny on one side of Tabitha, the detective on the other, Detective Shanley told them the details of how they'd found Jackson.

Tabitha hadn't been wrong when she'd seen that picture of Jason. Hadn't been wrong in believing she'd found her son. And she hadn't been wrong to have faith in Mallory Harris. As it turned out, Matt had been trying for a while to get Mallory to go out with him. The night after she'd first met Tabitha and Johnny in the pub, the night after she heard Tabitha's story, she'd finally accepted Matt's invitation. She'd spent the past week dating him to learn whatever she could about him. And so she could keep Jason close.

Mark was a smart man in a lot of ways. He was good at keeping his cover. But he'd had no idea Mallory had Tabitha's list. Not only had she been able to confirm all the likes, dislikes, mannerisms and idiosyncrasies Tabitha, with Johnny's help, had listed, she'd gone farther than that. She'd asked leading questions to trip him up. Had asked him if he'd been in the delivery room with his wife, and when Mark had said yes, she'd asked enough questions to realize he was lying. He didn't know enough about the moment-to-moment experience of childbirth to pull it off. Only someone who'd actually been in a delivery room would know.

The culmination had come when Mark told Braden he was taking off the anniversary date of his wife's death. He'd told Mallory that he was over his wife. That the relationship hadn't been working even before she died. There would have been no reason, then, for him to take time off from work to commemorate that date.

"So…did she confront him?" Tabitha asked. She seemed to be doing so much better, although Johnny knew she had to be dying to see her baby boy. At that point, he was eager to meet the young man himself.

Detective Shanley shook her head. "She called us and told us she was afraid she had a kidnapped toddler in her care."

"She called you this morning?" Tabitha asked.

"No, she called first thing yesterday morning. Your first warrant had already been denied, but our second attempt granted a warrant for DNA immediately and we took the swab without his father knowing. We were able to get a positive match with the sample you left with Detective Bentley a year ago. We've had them both under surveillance ever since."

"Where's Mark now?" Johnny had to know.

"He's been arrested and charged with kidnapping. A host of other charges will be following shortly, I'm sure."

"When can I see my baby?" Tabitha's question was no more than a whisper.

The detective nodded at a mirror Johnny suddenly realized had to be a one-way window. Seconds later, the door opened and Mallory Harris was there with a toddler in her arms, Braden right behind her.

"Oh, my God!" Tabitha's voice was soft, but filled with more emotion than Johnny had ever heard. He couldn't imagine the control it must have taken her to approach the child slowly. To wipe the tears from her eyes and keep them away.

"Jackson?" she said, reaching out a finger to the little boy's hand.

The toddler studied her, a half frown on his face. "You remember I said you were going back home to Mommy?" Mallory asked.

Johnny figured the entire situation was going over the toddler's head, but Jackson nodded.

"Do you want to go to Mommy now?" she asked.

Johnny held his breath.

Jackson nodded.

And Tabitha had her son back in her arms.

Needing to look away, Johnny caught Braden watching him. The other man met Johnny's gaze, apology clear, and Johnny nodded.

He was no longer needed.

The first month after Jackson's return would probably always be a haze to Tabitha. Certain moments stood out. Like the first time her son touched her face, reaching for the tears she'd shed when she'd first held him. The trip to the hotel to collect their things was a blur, as was the ride back to Mission Viejo in the car Johnny hired for her, driver and all.

He'd had to go get the truck off the street and take care of business in San Diego. He'd made it home late Saturday night. She'd hoped he'd stop in, but didn't blame him when he didn't.

She should've been asleep. But she'd been waiting to hear his car. To know that he was back. And she was having a hard time taking her eyes off Jackson for more than a minute. The first week she spent every night camped out on the floor of her son's room. He was in his crib, but she was going to have to start thinking about a toddler bed.

She'd taken a leave of absence from work; she had twelve weeks available to her and planned to take Jackson back to the daycare at the hospital when she did go back to work, just as she'd done before his abduction.

She took him shopping. None of the clothes in his

room fit. He needed age-appropriate toys. She took him to his pediatrician, cried when she heard that he was a completely normal and healthy two-year-old. One night she fed him peas just so he'd make a face and turn away, and then cried when he did.

Johnny had stopped by the day after they returned home, but he hadn't come in. He'd told her he was leaving, putting his house on the market and heading home to get back to the life of a corporate lawyer. He'd met his goal where the food truck was concerned. He wanted her to know that his first order of business was setting up the Angel's Food Bowls franchise and the nonprofit, with franchise fees going to the charity. He'd be keeping his original truck, hiring someone to manage and run it for him, and the money it made would also go to the nonprofit. He said he'd be in touch.

She'd hugged him. Cried a little. Kissed him one last time. And said she'd be waiting to hear from him.

And she was. Waiting. Some part of her would probably always be waiting for Johnny. She wasn't expecting to ever hear from him again, though—other than, maybe, to work at the nonprofit. But even then, whoever he hired to be in charge could get in touch with her.

The third week Jackson was home she made an appointment to meet with a therapist. She couldn't seem to let her son out of her sight and didn't want her paranoia to have a negative effect on him. From what she was told, her feelings were completely natural, given what she'd been through. They'd dissipate to some degree with time. And the fact that she was aware of them, doing something about them, probably meant there was no reason to worry. She'd loosen up.

In the meantime, it wasn't hurting Jackson any to have his mother's undivided attention. He missed his daddy, testimony to the fact that Mark had been good to his son, been loving with him, but as the days passed, Jackson asked for him less and less.

At the end of the third week, Johnny called.

"I wanted to see how you're doing," he said.

"Good. We're great," she told him. And spent the next five minutes gushing about everything toddler. Then she felt self-conscious for wasting the time of such a busy, important man. "I'm sorry," she said. "I shouldn't have gone on like that. It's just…it's good to talk to you, Johnny."

"There's no need for an apology," he told her, but he sounded different. More…professional.

She wanted to ask how he'd been. What he was doing. But didn't feel she knew this Johnny well enough to impose.

"Listen, I also wanted to let you know that the initial paperwork for the nonprofit is done and I need your signature on a few things. I was planning to send someone by with a packet if you're going to be home."

Jackson had left the blocks he'd been stacking and walked over to her. The smell that accompanied him told her he'd just filled his pants. And, judging by the expression on his face, he wasn't quite done.

"My signature," she repeated.

"I've named you executive director," he said. "For now, that's mostly going to entail signing documents, but once we're up and running, you'll have a staff working for you—"

"Wait!" Jackson looked up at her sharp tone, so she softened it as she said, "Johnny, a staff? I have nowhere to put a staff." Had the man gone bonkers? Forgotten, in three short weeks, what her life was like?

"And I work three twelves," she added inanely.

"Are you saying you don't want the job? The pay is

good and you can do a lot of the work from home, to begin with." He named a yearly sum that was triple what she made at the hospital. And would allow her to be home with Jackson.

She loved her job, but to help parents who were suffering as she had—there was no question.

"Of course I want the job, Johnny," she said. She just couldn't believe he was really offering it to her.

"I'll get the packet over to you this afternoon."

She was grinning. Nodding. Wanted to ask him if there was any chance he could deliver the paperwork himself, but knew he'd be far too busy to make the trip. With traffic, it could eat an hour or two out of his day. "Okay," was all she said.

And then, as he was ringing off, "Johnny?"

"Yeah?"

"Thank you."

He didn't ask what she was thanking him for.

She didn't elaborate.

Tabitha had another call from Johnny's area code shortly after that. It wasn't Johnny, though. It was his mother.

Anne Brubaker introduced herself as though it was perfectly normal for the billionaire mother of her former billionaire lover to be phoning. She was phoning because, with Tabitha's new position as executive director of the Angel's Food Truck nonprofit, *Don't Forget Me*, she felt they should at least meet. Johnny had told her about Jackson. He didn't seem to have mentioned anything else between them.

Including that she'd lived next door to him.

Or worked the food truck with him.

"I was wondering if you'd like to be my guest at a

charity fundraiser four weeks from Friday. It's a lunch event, but will last most of the afternoon," she said. "It would give you an idea of the kinds of things you might want to think about down the road, when *Don't Forget Me* is up and running."

Don't Forget Me. She'd cried when she'd read the name Johnny had chosen for the nonprofit. It was perfect. And so Johnny to know that.

"I…" How could she say no to her boss's mother? "I'm not sure I'd have anything appropriate to wear," she said, watching as Jackson continued to try to get a plastic truck to balance on top of a purple elephant, picking up the truck again and again as it kept sliding off.

She was learning a lot from her boy. About patience. About the ability to roll with the punches and still find happiness right where you were.

"It's not all that formal an affair," Anne was saying, "but I can have a nice day dress sent over for you."

She could imagine how much *that* would cost. But again, the woman was her boss's mother. Did she know that their new executive director had also slept with her son?

Jackson moved the truck farther onto the elephant's back. It slid off the other side. She couldn't go to the function. She'd have to leave Jackson. She had no idea how to refuse.

"John's arranged for a nanny to accompany us, and got a room in the hotel where the event is taking place. So that Jackson will be close by at all times," Anne said next.

At that point, Tabitha started to cry.

Johnny was watching out for her, just as he'd said he would.

Didn't he get that that only made being without him hurt more?

Chapter Twenty-One

Johnny made it exactly a month before he couldn't take it anymore. Barging into his father's office the day after his mother told him Tabitha had confirmed her upcoming appearance at a charity lunch, he paced in front of the older man's desk, waiting for him to get off the phone.

Alex's secretary had told him that while, yes, his father was alone, he was on an overseas call.

Business was important, Johnny conceded that. He didn't want to interrupt. But he couldn't just wait outside if Alex was engaging in small talk, either.

With raised eyebrows, Alex watched Johnny, completed his business—probably sooner than he would have otherwise—and dropped the phone into its cradle. "What's wrong?"

"Nothing," Johnny said, plopping down onto one of the expensive leather seats in his father's office. The cost of the damned thing could have made Tabitha's house payment for six months.

Alex gave him the eye. Not an "or else" look, but one that told Johnny his father knew he wasn't telling him the truth.

It was up to Johnny whether or not he chose to correct the lapse.

"I've found my passion," Johnny blurted, cringing as he heard himself sounding like a high school kid. Which was about how he'd felt for the past several weeks.

"Your passion."

"Yeah, you know, the thing you have to do, no matter what. The thing you're driven to do, even if you can think of a hundred reasons why it might not work."

Hands folded on his desk, Alex nodded.

"I've never felt passionate about anything before."

"You never had to. It all came easy to you."

"Doing yardwork for an entire summer, cleaning the house for another summer—those did not come easy to me." He wasn't in a congenial mood.

Alex seemed to sense that Johnny was serious. And that things were about to change.

"So...what is this passion? What does it entail? How much time off do you need?"

He'd just returned to work. He had no intention of taking another vacation so soon. "I don't need any time off."

His father sat forward, looking a bit tired as he smiled. "I have to admit I'm relieved to hear that."

"Why? Whatever made you think I was going to take time off?" He'd been handling his responsibilities and then some. Had closed two very lucrative deals in the month he'd been back, in addition to getting the Angel's Food Bowls franchise operation started. They already had three trucks outfitted, painted and awaiting final permits to get out on the road.

"You've been...different since you got back. Restless. It's been obvious to your mother and me that you aren't happy. I'd hoped the sabbatical would help you get beyond Angel's death, but if—"

"It's not Angel's death," Johnny broke in, feeling a twinge. He'd loved his wife. Truly loved her. He'd been turned on by her, but there'd been no passion, other than sexual, from him to her. He knew the difference now. "As a matter of fact, I want to get married."

Alex's jaw dropped.

"That's why I'm here," Johnny said, only realizing the fact himself as he shot up from his chair. He wanted to marry Tabitha. "I plan to ask Tabitha Jones to marry me and to let me adopt her two-year-old son. There's no father named on his birth certificate, so there shouldn't be any legal obstacle." Yep. That was it. He hoped to God the little guy liked him.

And that he was good with kids.

It was a challenge he hadn't yet faced.

Mark, who was in jail awaiting trial for kidnapping, was out of the picture. Probably forever.

"You want to marry Tabitha? The new executive director of *Don't Forget Me*? I was under the impression the two of you just met when you did interviews for the position. That you chose her because she'd been the parent of a missing child who found her son again."

He hadn't really interviewed anyone for the position. He'd lined up possible candidates for Tabitha to consider as her assistant. But he'd tell her about that later.

"I wasn't just involved with helping her find Jackson. I've actually spent the past year with Tabitha," he told his father as he headed toward the door. "She was my next door neighbor and helped me run the food truck."

He wasn't hanging around to chat. Right now he had a mission.

He'd finally figured out what it was and there was nothing...*nothing*...that was going to stop him from completing it.

For the first time in his life, he was driven from the inside out.

He hoped Tabitha was ready to deal with the results.

Tabitha took Jackson to work with her when she gave notice. She hadn't planned to stay long, but they ended up spending more than three hours in the cafeteria as everyone came down to see him, a few at a time. And to talk to her. When they left, she had invitations stretching out until Christmas for get-togethers and gatherings. And she knew that leaving the hospital wasn't going to be a goodbye. Her coworkers wanted to be in her life for the foreseeable future. And she was going to let them. She was not going to turn her back on love and friendship for fear of getting hurt. Being alone hurt more.

She noticed a new small black car in the driveway next door when she pulled into her garage. Probably a Realtor. Or maybe the new owner. If Johnny had put his house on the market, there wasn't a sign in the yard yet. But he might have sold it himself. Whenever she went outside, she tried not to look over there, dreaded seeing the proof that their time together was really over, but she'd known it would come.

"Ma! Ma!" Jackson was kicking his feet in the back, wanting out of his car seat. Unstrapping him, Tabitha tried not to think about that car. It looked expensive. Some kind of sports car. She wasn't really up on them enough to know one from another.

Not many fancy cars in their neighborhood.

"I eat," Jackson said, bouncing on her hip. She'd intended to take him straight into the house, but couldn't resist opening the garage door again and taking another look at the black car. If a Realtor was over there, maybe she could find out what was going on. How Johnny was doing. If anyone was interested in the house.

"I eat," Jackson said, more loudly, sticking his fingers into her hair. "Mama, I hungry. Hot dog!"

Her son knew his own mind. And had a healthy confidence in speaking it.

A man in an open dark trench coat and shiny black shoes stood on her front porch. His hair was short and her heart started to thud. Had Mark escaped from jail? Been released on bond? She'd been assured he'd be remanded without bail as he was clearly a flight risk. But...

The man turned and, for a second there, her breath stopped.

"Johnny?" His suit looked ungodly expensive. Superbly cut, it fit him to perfection.

He didn't come down the steps. She didn't go up them. Suddenly completely still in her arms, Jackson gaped up at Johnny.

"You said you have to believe to see," he told her. "Well, sometimes you have to see to believe. See me? I'm here." He leaned against the rail as though he didn't care that it was leaving a mark on his perfectly pressed coat. Arms folded, he stared down at her.

"Why are you here?" If he had another job to offer her, she'd consider it, but with all the research she'd been doing, she had a feeling *Don't Forget Me* was going to be a full-time venture and then some. She was itching to get started.

"I plan to stay here until you believe that I'm not leaving."

She took a step closer. Had he been drinking? "Johnny, you can't spend the rest of your life on my front porch."

She hadn't seen him in a month, was aching for his touch, and they were talking about her porch?

Jackson wriggled on her hip and she set him down. He knew not to wander far, but she didn't have to worry. He went straight for the porch steps.

Johnny was watching as Jackson took hold of the rail and put one foot and then the other on the first step. He could make it up just fine, but Tabitha moved behind him anyway. She was still at the fear-of-something-happening-to-him stage.

If Johnny had come by to spend the night with her, she was going to let him. No questions asked. He couldn't help that he came from a different world, just like she couldn't help loving him. So if she was the woman on the wrong side of the tracks he had to visit on the sly, she'd accept what he could give her.

She'd even been thinking about calling him and offering him the opportunity. But only if he wasn't involved with someone else. She wouldn't be the other woman.

Not that she thought Johnny was the type of guy who'd want that, anyway.

He'd taught her that she didn't want to be alone anymore.

And that if she was alone, she had only herself to blame.

Of course, he could just be there to offer her another job. She could be his charity case.

Jackson had made it up three steps. Had one more to go. Johnny seemed fascinated with his progress. One step behind her son, Tabitha could smell Johnny's cologne. Was surprised to find that it hadn't changed. He smelled the same as he had the entire time she'd known him.

Jackson got to the porch and stood there, staring up at Johnny. "Hi," he said.

"Hi." Johnny smiled down at him. And then looked at her, also on the porch now, just behind her son. "Hello,

Tabitha," he said to her in an entirely different tone. He didn't smile, but his gaze bathed her in warmth.

"Hi," she said back, smiling up at him. "It's really, really good to see you, Johnny. You want to come in? Can you stay for dinner? Or at least a cup of coffee?" He wasn't her Johnny anymore. Didn't have all day.

Was probably eating every meal from fine china these days.

"Jackson wants hot dogs," she added.

"I'd like to come in."

Pulling her keys out of her purse, she unlocked the front door, ushered her son inside and let Johnny follow.

Jackson went immediately to his high chair. "Mama, I eat," he said, patting the seat.

She looked at Johnny and hated that they were wasting what minutes they had together. "Hold on just a sec," she told him, already reaching for the toddler cookies she kept for emergencies, putting them on Jackson's tray, along with a sippy cup filled with milk, and strapping him in.

Then she turned to Johnny. "You want a cup of coffee?" She hoped he'd stay that long.

He shook his head. Came toward her. "I want you, Tabitha."

She wanted that, too. More than she could have imagined. But she had a son to think about, and a quickie wasn't going to do it after a month away from him…

"I want to marry you."

She stood there looking at him. "Have you been drinking?" She'd wondered about that earlier.

"I've never been more sober in my life. I found my passion, Tabitha, the thing that pushes everything else into second place. The one thing I can't live without. It's you. You're my passion."

"Johnny, I already decided I want to make love with you. I was going to call and beg you to come visit. You don't have to ask me to marry you." Was he forgetting that he came from an entirely different world? That he no longer lived next door?

It occurred to her then that the car she'd seen was probably his. Because he still owned the house?

"You don't get it, do you?" He came closer. Wrapped his arms around her. "You are my life quest, Tabitha, and I need my partner."

"But…"

Fear clogged her throat. Froze the blood in her veins. If they were partners for life and she lost him…

"You have to believe to see," he said softly. "Believe that no matter what, even if death parts us, we will always be together, Tabitha. My strength is your strength. And yours is mine. That's what partnership is all about."

She couldn't let him do it.

"But…you live in an entirely different world. I won't fit in. I'm not even sure I *want* to fit in. Your family certainly isn't going to approve of the fact that I'm not like you. I don't know how to behave in your world." The more obstacles she listed, the safer she felt. "And…isn't it too soon after Angel's death? You just got back, aren't used to living your real life without her. Without a wife. And there's Jackson. Do you even like kids?" She had more to say, but he'd put his lips on hers.

Tabitha wanted to pull away. Knew she should. But had to kiss him just for a second. Had to allow herself that bliss…

"Mo! Mama, mo!" Jackson's demand for more food brought her back to the present. To reality.

She wasn't sure how much time had passed.

She got another couple of cookies. Enough to get her through the next few minutes. Put them on his tray.

"There are a lot of reasons this could fail, Tabitha," Johnny said, shrugging out of his coat and throwing it over the back of a chair. He moved further into the kitchen. Opened her refrigerator. Took stock and then started taking things out.

It wasn't like he hadn't cooked there before.

"I could make you a list of all the reasons if you'd like," he said when she remained mute. She just plain didn't know what to do.

"But, instead, I'll give you the one reason it won't fail." Okay. She needed that.

Leaving eggs and bread on the counter, he walked over to her. Took her in his arms. "If you hate living in my wing of the family home, we'll get our own place," he told her. "We can knock down the two houses we already own and put up a bigger house right here for all I care. If you don't like socializing, we'll only go to the events we absolutely can't miss. If you hate the people, we'll spend most of our time alone. We know that works for us. And even if it's a struggle for both of us, adjusting and all, it can't be as bad as living without you."

"Why won't it fail, Johnny?" She needed a damned good reason.

"Because you only fail when you quit trying and I am never, ever going to stop."

Tears sprang to her eyes again. She'd cried so many of them in her lifetime. Most of them alone. Behind closed doors.

Maybe it was time to open her doors…

Could she do it?

In the past, she'd had no choice other than to go on alone. But she had a choice now. Dared she risk leaving what she knew, what she clung to, to have a chance at so much more?

She had Jackson back in her life. She had all she'd thought she wanted or needed. But she'd been so lonely. Missing Johnny every minute of every day.

"Will you marry me, Tabitha Jones?"

Shaking, petrified, she tried to say *yes*. Her throat was dry.

The word wouldn't come out. She tried, but she just couldn't get it out.

So she nodded.

* * * * *

COMING SOON!

We really hope you enjoyed reading this book. If you're looking for more romance, be sure to head to the shops when new books are available on

Thursday
23rd August

To see which titles are coming soon, please visit
millsandboon.co.uk

MILLS & BOON

MILLS & BOON

Coming next month

THE MILLION POUND MARRIAGE DEAL
Michelle Douglas

Sophie had had good sex before, but what she shared with Will wasn't just good. It was *spectacular*. She hadn't known it could be like this.

Not that she said that to Will, of course. It smacked too much of a neediness that would send him running for the hills. She didn't want him running for the hills. Not yet.

Not that they spent all their time in bed. They spent hours riding Magnus and Annabelle as he showed her all the places he'd loved when he was young. They explored the glens and the hills, traversed lochs and cantered through crystal-clear streams. They spent hours playing board games and watching musicals with Carol Ann.

But when they retired to their room each night — they made love as if they never wanted to stop. Not just once, but again and again. As if they couldn't get enough of each other. As if they were addicted.

It wasn't until Thursday, though, that Sophie finally realised how much trouble she was in. When Will told her he had to go back to London the next day. The depth of the protest that rose through her had her clutching the wedding folder she held to her chest. As casually as she could, she leant a shoulder against the bedroom doorframe to counter the sensation of falling, of dizziness. Loss, anguish and despair all pounded through her.

Will sat on the side of the bed, his back to her, pulling on his shoes, so she allowed herself precisely three seconds to close her eyes and drag in a breath, to pull herself together. 'No rest for the wicked?' she forced herself to ask, with award-winning composure.

He didn't move and she tried to paste what she hoped was a cheeky grin into place. 'I suppose I should be focusing on the wedding anyway. Nine days, Will. The month has flown!'

He turned, a frown in his eyes. 'Do you want to back out?'

'Of course not.' It was just… She hadn't known when she'd agreed to this paper marriage that she'd be marrying the man she *loved*. 'Do you?'

Continue reading
THE MILLION POUND MARRIAGE DEAL
Michelle Douglas

Available next month
www.millsandboon.co.uk

LET'S TALK
Romance

For exclusive extracts, competitions
and special offers, find us online:

f facebook.com/millsandboon

 @millsandboonuk

 @millsandboon

Or get in touch on 0844 844 1351*

For all the latest titles coming soon, visit
millsandboon.co.uk/nextmonth

*Calls cost 7p per minute plus your phone company's price per minute access charge

Want even more
ROMANCE?

Join our bookclub today!

'Mills & Boon books, the perfect way to escape for an hour or so.'

Miss W. Dyer

'Excellent service, promptly delivered and very good subscription choices.'

Miss A. Pearson

'You get fantastic special offers and the chance to get books before they hit the shops'

Mrs V. Hall